"Whatever h... firmly attached ... chainsaw," Sylvia said.

Dale closed his eyes in exasperation. Clearly he'd underestimated his opponent. Something he'd never done. He had thought she was responsible for the bad press, and once he called her on it, she'd back off and the situation would be handled, and he'd never have to see her again. But that was proving to be a major miscalculation.

"Do you have something you want to say?" Sylvia asked. "Because I have a very crowded schedule."

This woman was insufferable, and he would like nothing more than to knock her down a peg by kicking that soapbox out from under her. But he heard his mother's voice in his head—"*Fix this, we're counting on you.*" The last thing they needed was a constant stream of protesters once they began construction. He took a breath and winged it.

"Ms. Ramirez, what I'd like to propose." Dale scratched the back of his neck, searching for the right words. "Well, what I was thinking..." He cleared his throat, "What I had in mind—"

"Is there a point coming any time in the near future?" Sylvia asked.

Dale couldn't believe she was drumming her fingers on the desk. Who did she think she was, acting as if she didn't have the time for him?

Praise for Maria Lokken

"A striking debut. A contemporary romance full of power, community and most of all, heart. Maria Lokken is a natural storyteller and an author to watch."

~Magda Cavin

~*~

"A love story that could only happen in The Heights! Truly entertained by the world and characters Lokken created."

~Carly Duncan, author

~*~

"Maria Lokken delivers a heartwarming enemies-to-lovers romance I couldn't put down!"

~M. O'Neill

~*~

"Absolutely fabulous!! I was hooked within the first few pages. The back and forth between the 2 main characters drew me in from the beginning. Would definitely recommend reading!!"

~Sylvia Nygaard

~*~

"I loved this fun romance with a Latin flair."

~ Michele Dugan

Billionaire in the Heights

by

Maria Lokken

Billionaire in the Heights

Contact Information: info@thewildrosepress.com

Cover Art by *Diana Carlile*

The Wild Rose Press, Inc.
PO Box 708
Adams Basin, NY 14410-0708
Visit us at www.thewildrosepress.com

Publishing History
First Edition, 2023
Trade Paperback ISBN 978-1-5092-4910-7
Digital ISBN 978-1-5092-4911-4

Published in the United States of America

Dedication

To Rainer. Forever. You know why.
To Marisa, Claudia, and Eugene. And they know why, too.

Acknowledgements

As much as writing is a solitary affair, it's not done in a vacuum. This book would not be possible without the guidance of my editor, Leanne Morgena.

I'm also lucky enough to have two wonderful critique partners. Thank you to Magda Triantafylidou, and Carly Duncan, who I now call my friends. We're in this together.

Chapter 1

Dale Forester ran a hand through his dark hair, stretched his six-foot two-inch frame, and took his first deep breath since the day began. The city hall meeting room, with its old windows and poor ventilation, had become cramped and stuffy. Half-eaten donuts, empty coffee cups, and yellow writing pads now littered the oval conference table, barely accommodating both his legal team and the members of the city council. After two hours of droning legalese and hammering out the finer points of the contracts, Dale wanted nothing more than to make a hasty exit.

The mayor stood and stretched his long arms. He was as tall as he was wide. "Congratulations." His broad smile featured television-white teeth, and his bald head glistened under the lights. "I speak for the entire city council when I say we couldn't be happier to be in business with Forester Industries."

"Thank you." Despite his eagerness to get back to the office, Dale's easy charm and megawatt smile never wavered. He motioned to his legal team.

All four stood in unison and began making their way around the room, shaking hands with New York City Mayor Simms and the five members of the city council.

A strong hand clapped Dale on the back, and he turned to find a short, stocky man in his late fifties. He was a council member, but Dale couldn't recall his name. *Samuels? Santiago? Starts with an S. Oh, right, Sabina.*

"Mr. Forester, this will be great for the community. I'm glad we were finally able to make it happen." Councilman Sabina leaned in. "Honestly, I wasn't sure this deal was ever going to go through."

Outwardly, Dale's smile appeared confident, but the tightness in his gut told a different story—six long, pressure-filled months of touch-and-go negotiations.

"Excuse me, everyone," Mayor Simms called in his deep baritone voice, "my deputy has arranged a table at *Mangiare* for a celebratory lunch."

As much as Dale needed a moment to take in this big win, he didn't have the luxury of time. Too much still needed to be accomplished on this building project, and it had to be perfect. If he could complete the construction within the scheduled time frame and budget, the Forester board of directors would finally stop questioning his fitness to run the company. "We'd love to, Your Honor, but I'm afraid we must get back to the office." Dale glanced at his phone for the first time in an hour. "Rain check?"

Before the mayor could respond, the door flew open with such force it slammed against the wall, and a dark-haired woman in a bright-red blazer stormed in. In an instant, the room fell silent, and everyone's gaze focused on the intruder.

For a moment, Dale thought he might be the object of her fury.

Instead, she marched right past him and took a stance directly in front of the mayor.

Dale stared. *She looks familiar. Do I know this*

person? Before his mind could place her, the sound of her voice filled the room.

"This is low, even for you, Simms. Did you really think I wouldn't find out?" She pointed her finger at the mayor's chest. "What was it? A memory lapse? Or did you deliberately not tell *anyone* you changed the date of this meeting?"

The mayor's large frame backed up against the conference table. "Sylvia, you can't just barge in here."

"Actually, I can. And I did." She crossed her arms over her chest. "According to the city bylaws, these proceedings are open to the public. And *I'm* the public."

"Fine, but there's nothing you can do. Nothing is going to change." The mayor let out a long sigh. "The contract's been awarded and signed. It was decided weeks ago. You know that. This meeting was simply a formality."

For several minutes, Dale watched as if at a tennis match, as the mayor and the fiery, dark-haired woman traded barbs. Fascinating as it was, he'd gotten what he'd come for, and now it was time to leave. He grabbed his briefcase, nodded toward his team, and walked to the far end of the conference table toward the exit.

"You!"

Dale inwardly groaned. The last thing he wanted was to be the focal point of this drama.

"Yes, you and these…these…thieves over there"—she tilted her head toward the five council members huddled in the corner of the room—"have just ruined a neighborhood."

With those words, Dale had a light-bulb moment.

How had he not recognized her the minute she'd stormed in? This was Sylvia Ramirez, the chief instigator of a months-long protest against his proposed development. He'd avoided a face-to-face with her by sending his vice president of community relations to all the neighborhood meetings and rallies.

But the media photos hadn't done her justice. She was taller in person, he guessed about five feet, six inches, and her curly, shoulder-length hair wasn't just brown, it was the color of roasted chestnuts. Ms. Ramirez was stunning, even with a tight smile and clenched fists.

The written reports from his public relations and legal teams, however, had been dead accurate; this was not a woman who backed down or could be easily intimidated.

The council president, a tall man with a pencil-thin mustache, stepped forward. "Sylvia, don't do this. Not now."

"Actually, now is the perfect time." She waved him away and turned to Dale.

Dale felt the full weight of her anger as her gaze bore into him.

"In the event you've been living under a rock these last months, I'm the director of the Washington Heights Community Center, the one you've just signed a deal to tear down."

"I'm sorry, Ms. Ramirez. This is something you'll have to take up with your city council." Dale hurried toward the exit, desperate to get out of the room.

"Hold on," Sylvia said. "If you tear down the community center and go through with this development, the people in the neighborhood will have nowhere to go—"

"You're talking nonsense," the council president said.

"Am I? What about the senior citizens; where will they go for a hot meal? And the kids? If there are no more programs for them, they'll be left to hang out in the streets. Do you think that's a good idea? And what about my Girls Up scholarship program?"

Dale wasn't in the mood to defend a project that had already been contested and decided. Forester Industries needed this deal, and he had a responsibility, not only to the board of directors, but to the hundreds of employees who worked for the company. He turned to face her and tugged at his collar. "Listen, Ms. Ramirez, Forester Industries will bring a lot of good to the Washington Heights neighborhood."

"How?" Sylvia put a hand on her hip. "By building apartments no one around here can afford? Or leasing space to stores we can't afford to shop in? Is that how?"

"Ms. Ramirez, you're upset—"

"Mr. Forester, don't patronize me. If you're not prepared to include a new community center in your development, then the people in The Heights have no use for you, and we will continue to protest."

Dale clenched his jaw. The last thing he needed was more protests and bad press. "I'm sorry, Ms. Ramirez, this meeting is over."

"I'm not giving up."

"You should. Your community center is old and decrepit."

"The Washington Heights Community Center is an institution with a history of helping people," Sylvia said.

Dale gripped his briefcase. *Would this woman never stop?* "Listen, it was poorly constructed to begin with, and unfortunately, it's had no upgrades since. It needs a new roof, the pipes are barely working, the ventilation system is shot, and I could go on. That building wouldn't have lasted another year. We're doing you a favor."

Sylvia scoffed, raising her eyebrows. "You call destruction of this magnitude a favor?"

Dale closed his eyes. Clearly, getting through to her was impossible. He took a breath and pulled the contract out of his briefcase in the hopes this unscheduled confrontation would come to an end. "This document says we legally break ground in one month. Whether you protest or not. You can't do anything to stop us from building."

"That's where you're mistaken, Mr. Forester," Sylvia said. "You'd be surprised what I can accomplish in a month. And you're about to find out just how badly you've miscalculated."

****

Stepping off the treadmill, Dale looked out of the window and took a swig from his water bottle. Memories of the meeting in the mayor's office two days ago still haunted him. "She has to be the most exasperating woman I've ever met. And did I mention strong willed and stubborn?" He grabbed a towel and mopped the sweat off his forehead. "She did her best to ruin the most important day of my career." He glanced at the clock hanging on the wall of his home gym. "Well, aren't you going to say anything?"

Two quick barks were the only response.

"You're right. I'll ignore her." He tossed the towel

into the hamper and headed toward the shower.

These early morning, one-sided conversations with Mutt, his black-and-white mixed breed, helped him work out whatever was on his mind. And this morning's topic was the very attractive, but very obstinate, Sylvia Ramirez.

His legal team would have to deal with her constant phone calls, demands his contract be revoked, and threats of more protests. "Well, Mutt, I've decided today's a new day, and as far as I'm concerned, she no longer exists." Dale snapped his fingers in a *poof-she's-gone* motion.

Turning on the faucets, he stepped into the shower and let the hot water run down his back, easing his tension. *Completely erased from my mind.*

Thirty minutes later, dressed for the day, he entered the dining room.

The chef, a freckled-faced older woman, placed his usual breakfast of an egg-white omelet, black coffee, and a bowl of fresh fruit on the table. "Thank you, Gertrude." Dale sat and savored the first taste of his morning coffee. Placing the napkin on his lap, he reached for his tablet and pulled up his emails.

"The Buffalo project is back on target." He put Mutt on his lap and gave him a blueberry. "And we're up five points in the market." He scratched the dog behind his ear. "It all looks good. No major fires to put out. Let's see what's in the news, shall we?"

Mutt perked up, wagging his tail.

The web browser took a moment to open, and Dale poured his second cup of coffee. The news site barely finished loading when he sat forward and stared at the screen. "What in the…how…?" Stunned into silence, he took several minutes to scan the main story. When he came to the end of the article, he gritted his teeth. His only reaction was to scream. “Who did this?”

Mutt leaped off Dale’s lap and began barking, turning in tight circles and jumping up and down.

Gertrude poked her head into the dining room. “Is everything okay, Mr. Forester?”

“No, damn it!” Dale pushed away from the table and threw his napkin onto his plate. He stood and reached for his mobile phone, swiped it open, and pressed the speaker button. “Call Cunningham.”

The call was ringing through when his mother marched into the room. Her deep-blue cashmere dress accentuated her long, lean frame and highlighted her blonde chignon. “End the call, dear,” she said, keys dangling from her index finger. “I knew you’d be busy, so I let myself in.”

She bent down and picked up Mutt. “Aw-w-w-w, what’s the matter, my sweetness?” she cooed. “Did Dale scare you?” She held the dog against her chest and stroked his head with her well-manicured hand. “There’s a good boy.”

“Mother, you know you’re welcome here anytime, but I’ve got a situation, and it needs handling right now. So please, let me get to it.”

“Dear,” Candace Forester said, “the entire East Coast knows you have a situation. You’re splashed across every major news site, social media feed, and blog from Bangor to Boca Raton. You even made *Good Morning Today*. And I imagine you’ll probably be a hot topic on *Talking with Kate and Amy*.”

“How could this have happened?” He shoved his hands into his pockets. “Did you read the entire article?

It says I'm personally responsible for depriving senior citizens of a hot meal. I'm forcing children to play in the streets and destroying businesses that have been in the Washington Heights neighborhood for decades. They're saying I paid bribes to get the contract."

Candace shook her head. "I'm aware of what *they're* saying, and now *you've* got to fix it. You can't palm this one off on Cunningham."

"But he's the company PR genius."

"Yes, and he's very good at it." She placed Mutt on the floor and took a seat at the table. "But you're the face of the company now, and people need to know what Forester Industries stands for and hear it from a Forester."

Dale took in a shaky breath and began to pace. His mother was right. It all rested on him now. After his father's untimely death last year, Dale had been made CEO. He'd had a rocky start, trying to keep the company going while mourning the loss of the one man he admired and loved most in the world. There'd been several project delays and lost bids, and the company's value had plummeted. As of last month, the board had put Dale on notice.

The only thing that mattered now was holding on to his position. In no way would he allow someone else to run the company his father built from the ground up. But the constant barrage of bad press over the Washington Heights Community Center put it all in jeopardy. "This whole situation is difficult to wrap my mind around." Dale ran his hands through his hair. "I'm one of the good guys. You know I fought for a different type of development project. I wanted to build a new community center and allow for affordable housing.

But what could I do? The board voted against it."

With a sigh, Candace nodded. "You put up a valiant fight, but as long as Oliver Banks is a board member, he'll try to trip you up every chance he gets. Your father never trusted him."

Dale continued pacing.

"Honey, please sit." Candace motioned toward a chair.

"I can't. I think better when I'm moving." Dale covered the considerable length of the dining room from one end to the other several times before he stopped and turned to his mother. "Maybe there is something I can do."

Candance lifted a brow. "Tell me."

"I'm sure the lawyers would advise against it, but I'll call a meeting with Ms. Ramirez."

Chapter 2

Sylvia Ramirez headed toward the entrance of the squat, one-story Washington Heights Community Center where her best friend and co-worker, Randi Gomez, waited. "Here, I bought you a latte." She handed Randi the cup.

"Jeez, girl, why'd'ya have to spend four dollars? We have a coffeemaker in the office."

"I thought we needed a splurge."

"Uh-oh." Randi narrowed her gaze. "You only splurge when you're depressed. What happened now?"

Sylvia let out a sigh and lowered herself onto the steps.

Randi sat beside her.

"It's not like we didn't already have enough problems keeping the Center open. Now it looks like the funding for the Girls Up scholarships have mysteriously disappeared," Sylvia said.

"What do you mean *disappeared*? How does money disappear?"

Sylvia played with the rim of her cup and took in a deep breath. "I mean the money is gone. We had it, and now we don't."

"Hold up." Randi slid her sunglasses on top of her head, pushing back her purple-dyed bangs. "I'm not tracking with you. What exactly are you saying?"

"I came in early this morning, and there were

messages on the voice mail. They must've come in last night after we left. Obviously, they were trying to avoid speaking to me directly."

"Honey, I'm bi-lingual, but you're not speaking any language I understand." Randi frowned and rubbed her forehead. Who is *they*? "Start from the beginning and tell me exactly what happened."

Sylvia made a rolling motion with her free hand. "They were all calls from some assistant to an assistant to an assistant's assistant. And each call sounded like the last, as if they'd all been reading from the same script. 'We're sorry to inform you, after carefully reviewing our financial commitments...' blah, blah, blah." Sylvia's gut tightened at the thought. "After a while, I stopped listening because I couldn't think with it. I mean, I literally had to pick my face up off the floor. In all my years of fundraising, this has never happened."

Randi put her head into her hands. "What is this, dump-on-us week?"

"I wish I could say everything was gonna work out. But, honestly, I don't know anymore. It's not enough we're in this fight against the construction of the new development, but the scholarships, too? I'm not sure how much more I can take." Sylvia let out a long sigh.

Randi put an arm around Sylvia's shoulders. "Hey, girl. Come on, smile. We're alive, we're healthy, and we're smart. I forbid you to look like you lost a million dollars."

"But I actually *did* lose almost a million dollars." Sylvia barked out a laugh one might mistake for borderline hysteria.

Randi squeezed Sylvia's shoulder. "Well, you still

got me."

Grateful to have Randi by her side, Sylvia gave a half-hearted smile. She didn't know what she'd do without her. They'd been ride-or-die buddies since grade school and had seen each other through every high point, and all the extreme lows; the deaths of Sylvia's parents, Randi's ill-fated marriage and final, bitter divorce.

They'd been inseparable, even attending university together. During their senior year in Boston, they'd created a mid-term project for their Social Impact class, and the Girls Up scholarship program was born.

After graduation, they'd taken their proposal to potential corporate sponsors and secured enough funding to send seven girls to college that first year. The program became one of the Community Center's most important activities.

"You know," Sylvia said, "I can't stop shaking my head over this. I mean, we've been doing this for five years, and no one has ever reneged on a pledge. It just doesn't happen."

"Now, I'm totally tracking with you," Randi said.

"And don't you think it's funny, not ha-ha funny, but something's-not-right-funny, that two days after I tell off the head of Forester Industries, our corporate scholarship funding dries up?"

Randi sat up. "Ye-a-a-a-h, you know, you're right. It doesn't quite pass the smell test. Too much of a coincidence." She slumped back against the step. "But so what? What can we do about it?"

"Well, we can't let down these girls. It's not an option."

"Uh-huh. So, again, I repeat, what can we *do*?"

"I heard you. I'm thinking." Sylvia stared off into the distance. "If I could just figure out how to stop Dale Forester."

"Is that all? Pfft." Randi waved her hand as if she were swatting away a fly. "He doesn't stand a chance."

"I appreciate the vote of confidence, but—"

"Nuh-uh." Randi shook her head. "There's no time for 'buts.' We gotta stay positive." She stood, pulling up Sylvia with her and into a hug.

"Seriously, Randi, I'm a little worried. I'm not sure what the next move—" Sylvia stopped short and pulled away. "Don't look now, but there's a strange car across the street, just sitting there idling."

"Huh?" Randi turned halfway.

"I told you not to look." She grabbed Randi's arm, backing her away from the street.

"Why can't I look?"

"Maybe it's a drug dealer. I can't tell. The windows are dark."

"Oh, please." Randi rolled her eyes and faced the street, despite Sylvia's warning. "Wow! *¡Qué chévere!* That's one sweet ride. It's not every day you see one of those."

"One of what?" She couldn't understand what was *sweet* about the car.

Randi gave her a light punch on the arm. "A luxury Italian SUV that costs more than a house."

"How'd you know that?"

"Remember Victor? My ex? In addition to being crazy, he was also crazy about cars. I learned a few things." Randi rubbed her thumb and forefinger together. "You are talking some serious cash for a ride like that. I wonder what it's doing up here?"

"Who knows, but I'm asking Miguel to come out and take a look. If it's still here in five minutes, I'm calling the police." Sylvia grabbed Randi's arm. "Come on, let's get to work. We have to start dialing for dollars and solve some of our money problems." She hustled Randi up the walkway, and they entered the building.

Halfway to her office, she spotted Miguel, the Center's custodian, waving from the other end of the hallway.

"Sylvia, we've got a problem in the basement." The tall, youthful-looking man motioned for her to follow him.

"Shoot. I hope it's not the septic tank." Sylvia crossed her fingers.

"Looks like we're gonna need another cup of java," Randi said. "I'll get the pot going."

"Thanks. I'll let you know what I find out." Sylvia hurried down the hall, reaching Miguel in a couple of seconds.

"It's down here." Miguel held open the basement door.

Sylvia stepped onto the top of the landing and squinted down into the gloom; she couldn't see a thing. "Jeez, I forgot how dark it is down there."

Miguel flipped a switch on the wall, and a bare lightbulb illuminated a corner at the far end of the dank space. "Looks like we got a leak from that ceiling pipe." He pointed to his right.

Sylvia held on to the railing and leaned forward. "Well, it doesn't look so bad. It's hardly dripping."

Miguel scratched his head. "That's the thing. I'm not so sure it's nothing."

"Okay. Okay." Sylvia let out a resigned huff.

"Let's take a look." She pulled her phone from her back pocket and, turning on the flashlight, descended the stairs. When they got to the bottom, she stepped off into five inches of water. "Ah, shoot." She lifted one soggy espadrille and wrinkled her nose. "I *so* do not want to know what's in that water."

Miguel choked back a chuckle.

Sylvia pointed the flashlight in his face and gave him a death stare.

"Sorry," Miguel said.

"Move." Sylvia made a shooing motion with her hand and then hopped out of the water and back onto the bottom step. "This is definitely a problem."

"That's what I was saying."

"What are we going to do?" Sylvia tried to hide the defeat she felt.

"I have a buddy who's a plumber. He fixes my toilet all the time. Maybe he'll do us a solid."

"If you could ask him, that would be great." She shook her head, knowing this was one in a long list of emergencies she needed to handle. She hated to admit it, but Dale Forester had been right. This place was falling down around her. Miguel's friend could probably stop the leak, but it would only be a bandage. What they needed was major surgery. That, or a new building.

"Okay, you call your friend to get the pipe fixed. I'll make a few calls. I need to find some people who woke up this morning with a burning desire to part with their money and donate it to the center. By the end of this day, I intend to have a least one situation dealt with." Sylvia marched up the stairs, espadrilles sloshing with each step. Back in her office, she removed her wet shoes and was about to lay her head on the desk and scream.

Randi interrupted, rushing in and performing a salsa twirl. "We made the headlines!" She held up her tablet and pointed to an article on the screen. "It's too good to be true."

"Get a grip. Let me see what you're talking about." Sylvia took the tablet and began to scroll. It took barely a moment for her eyebrows to raise and her jaw to go slack.

In bold block letters, the headline screamed, *BILLIONAIRE PLAYBOY MAKES ANOTHER CONQUEST.* Smaller type beneath announced, *A Community Destroyed by Forester Industries' Latest Megaproject*. Featured under the headline was a color photograph of a tuxedoed Dale Forester heading into Le Rivulet, one of Manhattan's poshest restaurants, a tall, slender model on his arm.

"Wow. Just wow." Sylvia sat back and crossed her arms. "You know, I'm not surprised. I mean, seriously, what'd he expect? He's been splashed across every media outlet for years. He's such a poser."

Randi laughed. "Yeah, but he poses so well. I forgot how *guapo* he is. That combination of jet-black hair and green eyes makes a girl take notice."

"Oh, *puh-lease*. Take a real look. What do you see in this photo?"

Randi leaned forward and pursed her lips. "Uh, one fine specimen of a man?"

"No. Randi. That's not what I'm talking about." Sylvia slapped a hand on the desk. "Arrogance. That's what you see." The half-smile staring back from the screen reeked of condescension. She couldn't hide her sense of satisfaction that Dale and his company had finally been called out. After all, he was in the process of eliminating her Community Center, and for that, he deserved this and so much more.

Randi put her hands on the desk, leaned forward, and gave Sylvia a crooked smile. “Look, I get it. I’m just saying, even though he’s an arrogant farthead and we hate him, he’s still damn cute.”

“Can we please get off his looks? The only way he’d be attractive is if someone performed a lobotomy on his personality.” Sylvia picked up the tablet and continued to read the article.

Randi came around to Sylvia’s side of the desk and looked over her shoulder.

The story claimed Forester Industries had bribed city officials to win the bid for the Washington Heights development project.

“Look, Sylvia, you can read the rest later. There’s no way the city will take away the project from Forester Industries. Even if it’s true, I bet there are city officials involved, and in a few days, it will all be swept into some dark corner and out of sight. So, I think we ask him for help.”

Sylvia looked up at Randi, her eyebrows rising an inch. “What? Are you crazy?”

“Not in the least.” Randi sat on the edge of the desk, facing Sylvia. “He’s the one with the negative press, and he needs to look good. So, we hit him up for help, so he can look good again.”

“First of all, there is no possibility this guy will help us. He pretty much made that clear at the meeting with the mayor and the council.” She paused and caught her breath. “Second, this headline says it all. This is a bad man. There is no way I'm gonna get into bed with him."

"I'm not suggesting you get intimate with this guy." Randi wriggled her eyebrows. "I'm saying maybe do a little mambo. Y'know, a back-and-forth thing. You need something from him. He needs something from you."

"No. Absolutely not." Sylvia brushed one palm against the other several times as if wiping dust from her hands.

Randi crossed her arms over her chest. "Look, from what I understand, you practically threatened the guy. Like building his development would be at his own peril. So, *chica*, what you got up your sleeve? What danger could you possibly throw at him? Your soggy shoe over there?"

The morning wasn't half over, and it had already become a lemon of a day, and she didn't like lemonade. Sylvia sat back, sinking lower in her chair. Randi was right; she had threatened Dale Forester. But she hadn't a clue what to do next. For the first time in her life, she didn't have a solution.

Chapter 3

Dale Forester hadn't expected to sit outside the Washington Heights Community Center for over an hour, but the conference call with his project managers for the Buffalo Development had taken longer than expected. Hitting the End button on his dashboard phone, he got out of his SUV and headed toward the squat, gray building. With its corrugated roof and cinderblock walls it looked even worse than in the photos he'd seen.

Once inside, he discovered the entrance hall empty and the reception desk unstaffed. He drummed his fingers on the counter and checked his phone for emails several times while waiting. After five minutes, he gave up expecting any help and decided to find Sylvia Ramirez's office on his own.

He chose the corridor to his right and headed down the hall. Out of nowhere, a young boy darted past. Dale shouted for him to stop.

After giving Dale a quick glance over his shoulder, he continued running and disappeared into the darkened hallway.

"How is no one here to direct people?" *Damn it, he ran a multi-million-dollar company with hundreds of employees, so how hard could finding one woman be?* He was certain he'd seen her enter the building a few moments ago, and the place wasn't big. Dale gave an impatient snort and stalked down the hall, determined to open every door until he found Ramirez's office.

Peering into the first door on his right yielded nothing but a knot of teens huddled around a computer screen. Backing away and into the corridor, he tripped over an industrial-sized bucket on wheels. "Hey!" Dale righted himself and came face to face with a tall, dark-haired man who appeared to be in his early twenties. *Miguel* was embroidered in green lettering above the chest pocket of his gray coveralls.

"Sorry, man, I didn't see you coming out the door," Miguel said.

"Well, watch where you're going."

With a shrug, Miguel continued wheeling his bucket and mop down the hall.

"Wait," Dale called. "Can you tell me where I can find Ms. Ramirez?"

"You mean, Sylvia? Two doors down on your left."

"Finally." Dale turned and marched down the hall until he found an office with a sign that read *Director*. As he approached the open door, he spotted Sylvia at her desk, talking to the same woman he'd seen her with on the steps outside the center. They were now huddled over a tablet. He wondered what they were reading. Could it be the kickback article?

Whatever it was, he noticed the same fire in Sylvia Ramirez's eyes she'd directed at him in the mayor's office. Dale straightened, squared his shoulders, and clenched his fists, as if getting ready for a fight. "Impressed with your handiwork?"

****

"It's him," Randi whispered. "Even better looking

in person."

"You!" Sylvia jumped to her feet. "What do *you* want?"

"I came to find out how much they paid you for that article about me, which seems to have gone viral. I'm wondering why you would make such false statements?" Dale said.

"Me?" Sylvia put a hand to her chest. "What on earth are you talking about?"

"Well, let's see." Dale leaned against the door jamb, folding his arms and crossing one ankle over the other. "There weren't many people in the meeting at the mayor's office. You do remember the occasion? The first time we met? As I recall, only one person objected to the proceedings, and that person was you."

It took all her willpower to keep from leaping over her desk and wiping the smug look off his face. Instead, she drew in a slow, steady breath and crossed her arms over her chest, taking a stance that said *you will not intimidate me*.

He strode into her office and sat, uninvited.

His large presence made the space feel cramped. Sylvia's eyebrows rose toward her hairline. "Have you lost your mind?"

"Not in the least."

"Well, is it possible you've recently suffered a head injury?"

"I assure you, Ms. Ramirez, I am one hundred percent sane. I'm merely asking if this article is your doing."

Sylvia took another deep breath and sat ramrod straight at the edge of her chair. "Mr. Forester, I had nothing to do with this article." She emphasized each word, as if speaking to a child. "Don't get me wrong. I'm thrilled they've written some hard truths about you and your company, but I can't take credit. I only just laid eyes on it seconds before you barged in here."

"What they've written are lies. And I didn't barge," Dale said.

"Actually, she's right." Randi spoke for the first time since Dale entered the office. "You did kinda barge."

"And speaking of arriving unannounced, what are you doing up in this part of Manhattan anyway?" Sylvia asked.

Dale pointed toward the offending article displayed on her tablet. "Trying to find out why you did this."

"Are you hearing impaired? I had nothing to do with that. Nothing. No. Thing." Sylvia felt as if her head would explode.

"Then whoever is responsible is out to make trouble, and not just for me."

Sylvia's heart skipped a beat. "What do you mean?"

"While I'll admit the article is damaging to Forester Industries, it also states you're having trouble securing funding for your education program, and it may soon be terminated."

Sylvia did a double take and held up a finger to get him to stop talking. She hadn't gotten far into the article before Forester arrived.

Sylvia and Randi huddled over her desk, taking several minutes to scan through to the end of the article. He was right; the second-to-last paragraph mentioned her difficulty securing corporate funding. She shook her head and chewed on her lower lip. This kind of news could scare off other potential donors. Now, anyone who might have been willing to contribute would be suspicious as to why other donors had dropped out. Could this article be the reason her funding had mysteriously dried up? Sylvia looked up at Dale. "How did anyone know about the problem with our scholarship fund? And if you read this, then surely you must know I had nothing to do with it."

Dale sat farther back in the chair. "Ms. Ramirez, as you can plainly see, and by your own example, most people have the attention span of three minutes tops—"

"You're really something, you know?" Sylvia narrowed her eyes. "First you accuse me of doing something I didn't do. Then you insult me. You have no boundaries, do you?"

"That's not what I meant. What I'm trying to say is, the article is designed to get people's attention. The headline grabs them, and they read the first two paragraphs at most. They skim the rest. If that. Mission accomplished, damage to my company. The bit about your scholarships comes at the end. It's why I thought you sold them the information."

"You're making no sense." Sylvia gritted her teeth, working hard to control her temper.

"Don't you get it? You had nothing to lose because this center *is* coming down. So, I'd appreciate it if you'd stop trying to thwart me."

"Hold up. Whether we lose the center or not—"

"It's coming down." Dale's tone was emphatic.

Sylvia practically bled from biting the inside of her lip. She wanted to choke this guy. "I have thirty days, and I will continue to fight Forester Industries and the new development for each and every one of those days." She rose and extended an arm. "There's the door, Mr. Forester. I'd rush through it if I were you, before any pieces of this dilapidated building fall on your head."

****

Dale didn't move. No one had ever pointed to a door and told him to leave. Besides, he hadn't accomplished what he'd set out to do. He still needed to get Sylvia Ramirez on his side. Forester Industries had already experienced her capacity to create trouble, and the company couldn't afford any more unwelcome publicity. "I have no intentions of leaving."

"But this is my office. You're here uninvited. I'm asking you in the nicest possible way to please leave."

"Showing me the door isn't what I'd call a kind gesture," Dale said.

"She really can be very charming, especially when people are doing things for the center," Randi said. "If you wanted to, you know, make a donation, I bet that would help her mood."

Dale turned to Randi. Until now she'd been mostly silent, and he'd almost forgotten she was in the room. "Thanks for the advice." His voice was strained.

"Randi! He's the reason we're in this mess. I don't trust him, and there's no way I'm taking his money. Whatever he might give will come with strings so thick you couldn't cut them with a chainsaw."

Dale closed his eyes and huffed. Clearly, he'd underestimated his opponent, something he'd never done in the past. He had assumed she'd been responsible for the calamitous news article, and once he called her on it, she'd back off, maybe even offer to get a retraction. The situation would be handled, and he'd never have to see her again. But that was proving to be a major miscalculation.

With supreme concentration, Sylvia straightened papers on her desk, and then sat. "Do you have something you want to say, Mr. Forester? Because I have a very crowded schedule."

This woman was insufferable, and he would have liked nothing more than to kick that soapbox out from under her. But he heard his mother's voice in his head—"*Fix this, we're counting on you.*" The last thing his company needed was a constant stream of protests once they began construction. He took a breath and decided to wing it. "Ms. Ramirez, what I'd like to propose…" Dale scratched the back of his neck, searching for the right words. "Well, what I was thinking…" He cleared his throat. "What I had in mind—"

"Is there a point coming any time in the near future?" Sylvia drummed her fingers on the desk.

Unbelievable. This woman was insufferable. Throughout this entire meeting, she'd behaved like an impatient parent waiting for her child to finish his vegetables. Who did she think she was, acting as if she didn't have time for him? He tightened his grip on the armchair and glanced around the cramped, institutional-looking room. A poster on the wall to his left caught his attention. Held up with thumbtacks, it featured five stick figures in various colors, hands joined, forming a circle. The slogan, *Helping Hands Working Together,* was drawn in bright pink lettering underneath the illustration. The sentiment sparked the germ of an idea. Dale sat straighter. "I propose we…um…well, let's find a way to work through this situation together." He relaxed his grip on the armrests and sat back again, pleased with himself for shaping something out of thin air.

Of course, he didn't have a clue what this let's-work-together thing would look like. And frankly, it didn't matter. He needed her on his side. Maybe, despite her resistance, he'd find a way to make a sizable donation to her scholarship program, and that would be the end of her and her meddling. No more Sylvia Ramirez complaining about big bad Forester Industries.

But the silence in the room was audible, and he was positive this was the longest Sylvia Ramirez had ever gone without talking. "So, what do you think?" Dale prompted after several more moments. His question was met with stony silence. While he rather liked the sound, he had places to go, and he needed to get this woman's commitment. He pushed forward. "We can have our people work out the details."

Sylvia stood, clasped her hands together in front of her. "Mr. Forester. Thanks. But, no, thanks. And now this meeting is over. Good day."

Stunned, he fought to show any emotion. Dale had never been so thoroughly rejected by anyone. Clearly, he would need a different approach with this opponent. Keeping his expression neutral, he rose from the chair, nodded to Sylvia and Randi, and then stalked out of the room.

****

For several seconds, Sylvia sat motionless, staring at the wall opposite her desk. She took in a long, slow breath, and the tightness in her chest began to ease.

Randi pointed to the door. "You're letting him go? Just like that?"

"Uh-huh." Disgust ringing in her two-syllable response. "We're better off without him."

"You wanna tell me how we're better off alienating the guy who has the contract to tear down this place?"

Sylvia didn't answer. Instead, she walked to the only window in the room and stared out through the sagging blinds.

"Hey, don't blow me off. Tell me how we're better off letting serious cash walk out the door? For God's sake, girl, he's offering us help. Grab the lifeline." Randi slumped into the chair Dale vacated. "This is just crazy pride, and you know it."

"I'm not crazy. Trust me, those Foresters are all alike. I know the type. I've experienced people like him, up close and personal. Or have you forgotten? They have money, but no heart." Sylvia closed her eyes in an attempt to center herself and keep the memories of her ex at bay.

"I haven't forgotten," Randi said. "I was there, helping you pick up the pieces when Julian left. But I think this is different."

Sylvia shook her head. "No. It's not."

"*Ay, pobrecita*, I know you're hurting, but this is not the same." Randi went to Sylvia and gave her a one-armed hug. "This is business; it's not about a relationship. You're not gonna fall for this guy."

Sylvia stiffened. "I'm not remotely interested in him. But that's not the point. The point is, he can't be trusted. Look, I know you mean well, but I'm certain there has to be another way to get what we need that doesn't include him, or his money."

"Sorry, I don't think there is, and you just chased our last solution right out the door."

Sylvia had a queasy feeling in the pit of her stomach. Had she made a mistake letting Dale Forester walk out? She contemplated it for a moment and found she had no regrets. “Nope, he’s not the answer to our problems.”

They stood in silence and gazed out onto the street, watching Dale Forester climb into his big, black luxury SUV, the one that cost more than a mortgage on a house.

“What we witnessed was a hollow offer at best,” Sylvia said. “One way or another, we’d end up selling our souls.”

“Are you sure about that?” Randi asked.

Chapter 4

Dale threw his car keys on the desk, waking his computer screen. His inbox lit up, indicating dozens of messages from major media outlets. Clearly, he was this week's fodder for the twenty-four-hour news cycle in constant need of feeding. "Peter, would you come in here, please?"

A young man in tortoise-shelled, horn-rimmed glasses appeared in the doorway of the large corner office. "Yes, sir?"

"Candace is on her way. Can you order her usual?"

"A large vanilla iced mocha latte, extra vanilla, no whipped cream?" Peter tapped the order into his mobile.

"Yeah, and I'd like an iced coffee, black."

"Certainly, sir." Peter turned and left the office.

Dale blew out an exaggerated breath. "Damn. How did this happen?" Grabbing the back of his chair, he shook it several times before shoving it against his desk. The situation was unraveling on too many levels.

Over the last few months, he'd worked hard and done enough damage control to win a couple of big contracts and get Forester's share price moving in the right direction. But the board had given him only two years to completely turn things around, and he hadn't managed to accomplish that yet. He couldn't let Sylvia Ramirez's threatened protests of the Washington

Heights project put his position in further jeopardy. He couldn't allow her to hurt his father's company, or potentially put hundreds of people out of work.

Dale paced behind his desk for several minutes before abruptly stopping and picking up his phone. "Peter, give all the press inquiries to Cunningham to deal with." As he clicked off, his mother waltzed in.

"How did it go?" Candace asked.

Dale looked away and sighed.

"Oh, dear. That awful?" She crossed the room, placed her purse on the coffee table, and sat on the custom-made couch.

"Actually, it might be worse."

"What happened?"

Dale leaned against the edge of his desk and thought for a minute. What *had* happened? He hadn't really had a plan, just a vague notion he needed Sylvia to stop causing trouble. Then, without really thinking, he'd offered to help her, and to his shock, she'd turned him down. She was out of her mind. And he knew from experience, when someone had nothing to lose, they could do unexpected things. "To tell you the truth, I'm not sure what happened." Dale threw up his hands. "All I know is, several situations need handling on a right-now basis."

"Start with one." Candace sat back.

Before Dale could answer, his assistant knocked on the door and entered with coffees in hand. Dale motioned for him to put them on the table in front of the couch.

"Would you like anything else?" Peter asked.

"No, thanks. This is great." Dale picked up his coffee, dispensed with the straw, and removed the plastic lid. Closing his eyes, he took several large swallows, savoring the burnt-chocolate taste and cool iciness as it went down his throat.

“Do get on with what you were saying, dear.”

“Right.” Dale cleared his throat. “Well, there’s a clause in the Washington Heights Development contract which states if we don’t start building in a month, we lose the job.”

Candance arched her brow and leaned forward. “So, what’s the problem? Aren’t we ready to move? Surely the plans and permits are in place?”

“Yes, everything is set to go. The problem is Sylvia Ramirez.” Dale began pacing, as the effect of the caffeine worked its way into his system. “She’s threatened to organize neighborhood protests against us the entire time we’re in construction.”

Candace’s eyes widened. “But that would be a disaster.”

Disaster didn’t even begin to cover what Dale would be facing if those protests caused major construction delays. He had no doubt the board would oust him as CEO, and he could not let that happen.

While he didn’t know his next move, he knew it would have to include convincing Sylvia Ramirez to change her mind. And he dreaded the thought.

****

The lunchtime crowd had thinned, and Sylvia and Randi were sitting at their usual table in their favorite restaurant, *La Cocina*. The owners, Carmen and Luís Alonzo, had been friends of Sylvia’s parents. The eatery was one of the best in the neighborhood, and on a Saturday night, or a Sunday after church, a line of hungry people could be found waiting for a table.

What Sylvia loved most about the place was the delicious aromas filling her senses the moment she walked through the doors. It reminded her of her mother's kitchen at holiday time. When her parents were alive, they'd eat family dinners here at least once a week. Now, it was one of the places where she could sit and think, with a *café con leche*, or a pastry, or have a quiet dinner without being bothered.

Randi snapped her fingers in front of Sylvia. "Hell-ooo, where'd you go?"

"I was thinking about my parents. If they were here, we'd have a completely different fight on our hands. They would have already had this handled." Sylvia slumped back in her chair. "I'm such a failure."

"No, you're *not*. We just gotta think like them. There's something we're missing."

Both of Sylvia's parents had been lawyers at the Legal Aid Society in Manhattan. They taught her to take a stand for what mattered, and to help people in need. She was certain they would have come up with a solution for the community center. It pained her to think how devastated they would have been if she didn't fight against a development that effectively shut out the people in the neighborhood. "I miss them." Sylvia sniffled.

Randi sighed. "I miss them, too. But it's up to us now, and it's been two days since Dale Forester made his offer to help. *Tick-tock*." She pointed to the non-existent watch on her wrist. "What are you going to do?"

Sylvia shook her head and gazed out the front window of the restaurant. "I'm still not going to take him up on his offer."

"¡Tú eras una mula!"

She faced Randi and lifted her chin. "I am not a mule."

"Yes, you are. Seriously, you might want to check that."

Sylvia scoffed. "Please, being stubborn has served me well. Besides, his offer was too vague."

"It was not." Randi slapped a hand on the table.

"Oh, spare me the dramatics. His offer was translucent. You could see right through it, because there was nothing there. *Let's work together.* What does that even mean?" Sylvia pursed her lips and leaned forward. "It had V-a-g-u-e written all over it."

"However translucent, vague, see-through, or otherwise it might be, it's got to be better than the dead end we're looking at."

Was she really out of options? Sylvia thought for a moment. All her life, she'd been the girl with a multitude of scenarios up her sleeve. If Plan B didn't work, she'd go through the whole freaking alphabet until she found something that would. "Honestly, Randi, I was certain we'd either get a reprieve, or someone would come through with a new building." She picked at her salad. "I guess I was hoping for a miracle."

For months, Sylvia tried to get the city to recognize that any plan for a new development would have to include a new Washington Heights Community Center. But she'd lost that battle; the only thing the city council was working toward was the gentrification of the neighborhood, including retail stores that would pay considerably more money in taxes to the city. She put down her fork. "I'm kinda out of solutions."

"Well, then, we might have to put aside our pride and our prejudices." Randi's hands took on a prayerful pose. "Please, I'm begging you; forget the past. Forget your ex. Let's grab a hold of the floaties Dale Forester is offering. Anything is better than what we've got."

Sylvia chewed on her lower lip, lifted her face toward the ceiling, and let out a groan. "No. Just no." She stared a Randi, who looked as if she were about to cry. "I'm sorry. I can't. I hate everything he stands for."

Her phone rang, and she checked the caller ID. "It's Miguel." She swiped open the phone. "Hey, what's up?"

"We got a—"

"Talk louder. I can hardly hear you." She pulled the phone closer to her ear and pressed her palm against the other.

"I said, we got a situation," Miguel said.

"What? What happened?" She stared into Randi's widening eyes. They seemed to mirror the anxiety creeping up her spine.

"A pipe burst in the basement. You need to get back here right now."

"How did *that* happen?" Sylvia asked but received no response. "Hello, Miguel, are you there?" She pulled the phone away from her ear, only to find the screen saver photo of her parents staring back. "He hung up."

It took less than ten minutes for Sylvia and Randi to pay their bill and race the few blocks to the center.

Miguel was sitting on the front steps with his head in his arms folded on his knees.

"Oh, man. That's not a good sign," Randi said.

Miguel looked up. "It's a mess. I've shut off the main valve, but water's still coming in."

"How's that possible?" Sylvia hadn't thought things could get worse, and yet, here she stood in the middle of yet another problem.

Miguel shrugged. "It's an old building, you know, with additions and add-ons and lots of cheap labor. It could be another valve not connected to the main one. I don't know. I'm not a plumber."

The squeals of children playing in the spray of water shooting out of an open fire hydrant filled the air. Sylvia took in a breath and looked up and down the block. The temperature was so hot the pavement shimmered. If she didn't know any better, she would have thought it was a typical summer day in the Heights, except for the fact everything in her universe was crumbling.

"So, what do you want me to do?" Miguel asked.

They were all relying on her, and all she felt was a sense of dread creeping up her spine and spreading across her body like branches of a tree. Her knees weakened, and she had to force herself to keep standing. "Okay. Look. This is just another problem we need to fix. And we'll fix it." Sylvia kept her voice calm and controlled, as if this were no big deal, which was as far from the truth as one could get. "Miguel, please go back to the basement. Give it one last look, and see if you can find the source of the leak. I'll be there in a second." She turned to Randi. "Let's put signs up on the bathroom doors to make sure no one uses them until we can figure out what to do."

Twenty minutes later, Sylvia and Randi had managed to tape up *Out Of Order* signs at all the bathrooms and the kitchen area.

Leaving Randi to source a plumber, Sylvia headed

toward the basement to check on Miguel and see for herself what was going on with the pipes. Moments later, she opened the basement door. "Man, it's dark down there." She flipped on the wall switch at the top of the landing, but the bare bulb at the base of the stairs remained dark. She flipped the switch up and down in quick succession several more times, but still no luck. "Seriously? This day just keeps getting better."

Standing at the top of the landing, she took off her shoes, pulled out her phone, and headed down the stairs, using the phone's flashlight to illuminate the way. "Miguel, you down here?" No response. "Hey, Miguel." Again, nothing. She continued down the steps. When she reached the bottom, she pointed the flashlight to the right and left. "Mi-gue-elllll, where are you?"

Sylvia shook her head and dropped her shoulders. Miguel was probably upstairs in one of the bathrooms looking for the leak. Since she was already down here, she thought she might as well have a look for herself.

From where she was standing, six inches of water appeared to cover the floor, and the level did seem to be slowly rising. It only confirmed what Miguel had said. Another pipe somewhere was still contributing to the flood.

Gingerly, Sylvia walked through the water, not knowing what her bare feet might step on as she headed farther into the semi-darkness. Every few steps, she pointed her phone's flashlight over the exposed pipes in the ceiling in the hopes of finding the source of the leak. The farther into the bowels of the basement she waded, the tighter the knots in her stomach became.

She passed several broken desks and chairs pushed up against the wall on her right, all in need of repair, and farther along, boxes and boxes of holiday decorations with water inching its way up their sides. "Shoot, I got a flood, a missing janitor, and a waterlogged basement filled with stuff that should have been thrown out years ago. This is *so* making my day. Miguel!" This time her yell was short and several decibels louder than before. As she trudged toward the back of the basement, she unexpectedly brushed her foot against something in the dark water to her left. She looked down and jumped back on a gasp. "Oh, my God. Miguel!"

Chapter 5

Dale was in the middle of his weekly squash game at the New York Racquet Club when he heard a knocking on the glass wall behind him. He turned to find Maddy, the perky, blonde front-desk receptionist waving for him to step out of the court. He tapped on his watch, as if to say, We still have another fifteen minutes of court time.

Maddy shook her head and continued motioning with a wave of her hand.

"Sorry, man." Dale shrugged at his squash partner. "Let me see what this is about." He grabbed a towel and wiped the sweat off his face. Pulling open the glass door, he stepped halfway out. "Hey, Maddy, what's up?"

The receptionist fiddled with the employee badge clipped to her waistband. "I'm sorry to disturb you, Mr. Forester, but your mother is on the phone at the reception desk, and she *insisted* I interrupt you. She says it's urgent she speak with you."

Dale blew out a breath and turned back into the court. "Hey, Ron, this will only take a minute." He jogged down the hall and up the steps toward the front of the club. Once at the reception desk, he picked up the proffered phone. "Mother, what's happened? Are you all right?"

"Yes and no," Candace said. "We have a situation.

It appears…well….as I said…"

"Mother," he interrupted, "are you sure you're okay? You don't have a terminal illness you forgot to mention?"

"Don't be silly, dear. It's serious, but nothing like that."

"Then why call me at the club?"

"Because I couldn't reach you on your cell."

"I was in the middle of a squash game, and my cell is in my locker. All I have is my racket. Why would I need my phone?" Dale took a deep breath. He loved his mother, but she sometimes took the long way around to get to the point. "Why don't you tell me what's got you so upset?"

"Well, she's at it again."

"Who is?" He shifted his weight from one foot to the other.

"Sylvia Ramirez. She's managed to capture the attention of that tabloid news program, what's it called? Oh, I can't remember the name. It's all letters, like the alphabet. XYZ, or WQY, or…oh, never mind. Anyway, the name of the program isn't important. What's important is they reported a story, and now everyone's running with it."

"What story are you talking about?" Dale's pulse quickened. He put his forehead in his hand, hoping she'd get to the point sometime soon.

"The flood in her community center. And the poor man who fell off a ladder and broke his arm, and now the story is everywhere, and—"

"Whoa, whoa, whoa. I have no idea what you're talking about, Mother."

"That's what I'm trying to explain, dear."

"It might be faster if I get an Internet connection. I'll call you back." Dale hung up, ran down the stairs to his locker, and grabbed his mobile from his gym bag. He quickly accessed the gym's Wi-Fi and began a search for *Sylvia Ramirez, Washington Heights Community Center.* The first page featured a dozen hits, each with a video. He lowered himself on the bench in front of his locker, pulled up a clip, and pressed Play. Holding his phone horizontally in both hands, Dale leaned forward, rested his elbows on his thighs, and let out a low whistle. "Wow."

He hadn't expected to find Sylvia Ramirez surrounded by a group of twenty senior citizens and two dozen children huddled in front of Presbyterian Hospital holding candles, flowers, and signs saying, *God Bless Miguel. Get well soon. We love you, Miguel.* "Who the hell is Miguel?"

The video cut to a close-up of Sylvia with several microphones surrounding her as she spoke to reporters. On the bottom third of the screen, a banner proclaimed, *Forester Industries Offers No Help.*

Dale stared open-mouthed. He thought her choice of a white sheath dress with her chestnut hair swept up in a high bun made her look angelic. "Smart move, Ms. Ramirez." Dale brought his phone closer and squinted at the screen. "Are those tears in her eyes?" He slapped the bench. "My God, she's a PR nightmare." Dale pushed the button on the side of his phone, raising the volume as the reporters asked questions, and Sylvia embellished her plight.

"Miss Ramirez, can you tell us what this vigil is about?" asked one reporter.

"We're all here praying for Miguel. He's the

custodian of our community center. Today, he tried to fix a burst pipe in our basement. Instead, he fell and broke his arm and several ribs." Sylvia brushed a tear from her eye.

Dale scoffed at the screen. "Oh, please. Spare me the theatrics."

"And how is he doing now?" A second reporter asked.

"He's resting comfortably, thanks to the good doctors and nurses here at Presbyterian." Sylvia pressed a hand to her chest. "But what happens when he gets out? He won't have a job because we're being forced to shut down the center."

A third reporter thrust a microphone in Sylvia's face. "Weren't you going to be closing your doors anyway?"

"At last, a sensible question." Dale blew out a breath. He didn't know how much more of this melodrama he could stomach. Despite the throbbing headache forming at the base of his skull, he couldn't turn away. His company's reputation was at stake, so he forced himself to keep watching as Sylvia continued to speak.

"We knew Forester Industries had been awarded the development contract, but they assured us we'd have at least the next month to continue serving the community and to come up with a plan to help the kids and senior citizens who rely on the center." Sylvia turned to face the camera, and her eyes were filled with tears. "Now, I don't know what we will do."

The picture cut away from Sylvia back to the reporter, who rehashed what had already been written about Forester Industries.

Dale stopped the video and put his head in his hands. Acid churned in his stomach, and he took slow, deep breaths working to push down his anger. How had she made this about Forester Industries instead of the dilapidated building and that poor custodian? Sylvia Ramirez was better at this than any politician he'd ever met. She'd manage to twist the interview to her advantage. He lifted his head, closed the browser on his phone, and shot off a text to his mother.

—Saw it. On it. Heading back to the office in 15.—

Jumping up from the bench, he tore off his shirt and shorts, his mind spinning as he headed toward the showers to wash off the sweat and clear his mind. Tilting back his head in the stall, Dale let the hot water run over his face as images of Sylvia at her impromptu press conference swirled through his mind. He'd known Sylvia Ramirez was shrewd, but he never imagined she would stoop so low as to turn a tragic accident into a media circus. That stunt just gained her all the public support she needed to put pressure on his construction project. Because of her, no one would think well of him or Forester Industries.

He turned off the water and leaned his forehead against the cool tile. Within a week, she'd gone from being a thorn in his side to a saber in his solar plexus. Somehow, he had to stop her. "She has no idea whom she's dealing with." His words, spoken through gritted teeth, echoed in the tiny stall.

As he toweled off, he tried to formulate a plan. He needed to act fast. Another round of unwelcome publicity would ensure Forester Industries' share price would go into a free fall. With a surge of energy, he moved into the dressing area, more determined than ever to put a stop to her. "Does she truly believe she can get away with this?" Dale's voice rose as he banged the side of his locker with a fist.

Two other members in the room gave him a wide berth, quickly gathering their rackets and leaving.

"She has no idea what money can buy, and I am just the person to show her. She'll regret the day she started this." He continued to dress while talking to himself like a football coach firing up his team on the day of a big game. Adrenaline flowed through him, and his heart beat faster as he pictured squashing all her efforts. First, he'd attack her with a lawsuit. Then he'd bury her with enough legal torts she wouldn't be able to take a breath, let alone protest his development. "Now we're talking."

Dale grabbed his tie from the hook inside the locker and strung it around his shirt collar. He strode to the mirror to make the knot, but his reflection forced him to take a step back. He didn't recognize his face. His eyes gleamed with hatred, and his mouth was twisted in a snarl. When had he become this mean and ruthless?

Dale took several more steps back, loosened his tie, and reached for the wall to steady himself. Closing his eyes, he inhaled; an image of his father flashed in his mind. He shook his head, trying to rid himself of the picture, but it wouldn't budge. He opened his eyes, hoping it would make him feel better. Instead, only a deep ache remained, as if he'd been punched in the gut knowing how ashamed his father would have been of him at this moment.

The man who had been his mentor and best friend would have been deeply disappointed.

Dale looked in the mirror again and asked himself a question he hadn't thought of in years. *What would Dad do?* Lowering himself onto the bench, he put his head in his hands and softly wept.

When Charles Forester was alive, the company put the community's needs above any company project. He could hear his father's voice, "Son, we're here to make things better for everyone and not only to create profits for the company. How you treat others and what you do for them will define who you are."

When had he forgotten that concept? When the board voiced doubt about his ability to run the company? Or was it Oliver Banks opposing him at every turn? They certainly hadn't made it easy, giving him only two years to prove himself or be replaced.

He shook his head. It didn't matter. None of it mattered anymore. He knew if his father were alive, Dale could offer no defense for his behavior over the Washington Heights project. He'd done things out of fear of losing his position. "Damn it." Dale wiped his eyes and took in a slow breath.

With memories of his father fresh in his mind, he finished dressing. He had some changes to make and hoped he was up to the challenge. The time had come to be the kind of CEO his father had intended him to be.

Chapter 6

Dale exited the club and climbed into the waiting company car. The ride to the office gave him time to think about his contemptuous relationship with Sylvia Ramirez. After everything she'd done to malign his business, he accepted they would never be friends. But to truly honor his father's legacy, he would put aside his personal dislike and look at the bigger picture, beginning with helping the community in Washington Heights.

The first order of business would be changing Banks' sway over the other board members by creating a new plan they couldn't argue with. Months ago, he'd initially presented to the Forester board a plan which included a community center and affordable housing units, only to have it rejected by Oliver Banks. At the time, Dale suspected Banks was up to something but had no concrete evidence. And as Banks was the single most powerful board member, Dale hadn't fought him. Being CEO had sometimes meant shutting up and kissing up to Oliver or risking losing it all.

Not anymore.

Newly energized from his locker room epiphany, he called an emergency meeting with his top executives. Together they would move a small mountain quickly. One hour later, Dale stood at the head of the long, oak conference table, adrenaline pulsing through him like a caffeine rush as he waited for his team to arrive.

Seven executives entered the room one by one, representing planning, finance, construction, urban planning, design, production, and public relations. Each one was carrying a laptop, a tablet, or a yellow pad. Several not-so-subtle sideways glances slipped his way, as they took their seats around the table.

Dale pocketed his phone and cleared his throat. "Thank you all for coming on such short notice. I know you're aware of what's been happening with The Washington Heights development project."

Head nods and murmurs circled the table.

"Good. Then we can agree it's far from ideal, and if allowed to continue, it will cause major problems in the future." Dale shifted his stance and looked down. "Truthfully, the company is in a real predicament, but I believe it can be rectified if we revise the original development plans."

He took in a breath and looked up. Emotionless, blank faces stared back. Not the reaction he'd expected. A tickle of panic teased at the edges of his mind, and he tugged at his shirt collar. Despite the deadpan faces, he pressed on. "The original plans included a community center and affordable housing units. If we can push that plan through, everyone wins. To do that will take the efforts of everyone at this table."

Jason, the long-faced Chief Planner, spoke. "But that proposal has already been rejected by the board."

The others at the table nodded.

Dale strode to the window. He looked out at the traffic-filled avenue below and took a moment to think.

Except for Jason's pen tapping against his notepad,

silence filled the conference room.

"The plan failed because the board didn't buy into it." Dale turned to face the team. "It wasn't good enough. So, here's what's going to happen." He spread out his arms. "You're all here to help create a more compelling proposal. Because the company and the community need this development, and you're the people to make it happen."

"What's the timeline?" Marion, the Chief Architect, asked.

"Yesterday," Dale said.

The room gave a collective chuckle.

"Seriously. What's the timeline?" Marion smiled and tucked her grey bob behind her ears.

Dale leaned forward, pressing his knuckles on the conference table. "Yesterday." The single word was said with finality.

Marion's eyes widened.

Jason coughed.

"I need to present this to the board tomorrow. It cannot wait. We're headed toward a PR disaster if we don't turn this around, and I'm counting on all of you." Dale pointed to each person in the room. "So, cancel whatever calls, meetings, or dinner plans you have. We'll be rolling up our sleeves and ordering takeout."

No one at the table moved. Or spoke.

Dale hadn't expected such a chilly, non-committal reception. He pushed off from the table and crossed his arms over his chest. "Okay, so what's the problem, people? I'm sensing you're not fully on board with this. Am I right?"

A stocky man, sitting at the far end of the table, raised a hand. "May I speak frankly?"

"Cunningham, you're head of Public Relations. I'd expect nothing less."

"If we don't have Oliver Banks on our side"—Cunningham shrugged—"I'm not sure it matters how hard we work. He's already knocked the plan down once. What makes you think he'll agree to it now?"

Dale pursed his lips. They were making him work for this. "I know," he said. "But I believe we need to tweak the proposal and show Banks how this will benefit the company."

Marion shook her head. "I worked alongside your father for years, and even *he* had a difficult time with Oliver. Sometimes it took months to get his agreement on a project. He has a great deal of influence over the other board members." She hesitated. "I…well…I don't know how *you* plan to get him to agree to this."

Marion's downcast gaze was like a punch in the gut.

The other members of the team looked anywhere but at him.

A trickle of sweat fell down his back, and he chewed on the inside of his cheek. His lack of leadership, playing it safe, and kissing up to the board had put him in a place where even his senior management team no longer believed in him. Dale took off his suit jacket, draped it over the chair, loosened his tie, and sat. "It's painfully obvious I've lost some of your trust. But, let me ask you all a question. Is this a project you want to fight for?"

"Yes," Jason said.

The others at the table nodded.

"This is exactly the kind of project your father would have loved to work on."

"Jason's right," Marion said. "Once a year, we worked on a project like this. And yeah, they were hard but infinitely rewarding." She looked around the table. "Am I right? I mean, we did love it. Late nights and all."

"Yes," the other six in the room said simultaneously.

The pressure in Dale's chest eased. "Well, then"—he slapped a hand on the table—"we're going to have to pitch a revised proposal hitting all the points, so no one on our board can disagree. And I promise you, we can do this if we work together." Dale stood. "So, team, are you ready to try?"

Cunningham raised a hand in the air. "May I ask a question?"

Dale swallowed hard, hoping his head of PR wouldn't make this meeting more difficult by presenting a roadblock. He nodded. "Go ahead."

"Should we order Chinese? Or you want Mexican?"

Everyone laughed.

Dale's back muscles relaxed, and he smiled as he leaned back against his chair. "I say we order both, and don't forget the beers."

The team labored all day and long into the night, reviewing the original plans for the development. Together, they'd managed to write a better, more robust proposal and were confident the board would agree.

****

When Dale finally arrived home, it was past midnight, but he was too exhilarated to sleep. Instead, he took Mutt for a walk. They'd gone about twenty blocks down Fifth Avenue along Central Park when

Mutt parked his butt on the sidewalk and refused to move another paw, as if he were saying he'd had enough exercise and fresh air. Dale pulled on the leash, but Mutt wouldn't budge. "Hey, boy. What's going on?" He picked him up. "You tired?"

Mutt barked and licked his face.

"Yes, yes, I love you, too." Dale scratched him behind the ears and looked straight into his eyes. "You know what? We devised a scathingly brilliant plan to get us out of the mess we're in."

Mutt barked several times, wriggled out of Dale's arms, and took off for home, almost dragging his guardian down the street.

"Okay, boy, slow down. I'm coming." Dale laughed for the first time in weeks. Once back in the apartment, he went straight to his study and worked until three in the morning to put last-minute touches on the new proposal.

At dawn, he woke with a smile. Stepping into the shower, he began to whistle. The weight he'd been carrying around for too long had been lifted, and he felt exhilarated. He'd spent so much time proving himself to the board, he'd lost himself. With only six months left on his board-stipulated trial-run, the time for walking on eggshells was over.

Dale checked his reflection in the hall mirror before leaving for the office. An uninvited thought popped into his mind as he pulled his tie knot snugly against his collar. Had it been foolhardy to call an emergency board meeting to reverse a decision they'd already made? Or had it been a bold move? Dale shrugged. He was about to find out.

****

At one o'clock, Dale greeted Candace Forester and three others as they entered the wood-paneled, high-ceiling boardroom and took their seats at the large mahogany conference table.

A screen mounted on the far wall featured the remaining eight board members joining via teleconference from their respective locations.

When everyone appeared to be situated, Dale took his place at the head of the conference table. "Good afternoon. Thank you all for taking time from your busy schedules." He paused and tugged on his jacket. "My assistant, Peter, is passing out charts and financials to those present. Those who are remote, you'll find the information by clicking the paper clip icon on the bottom right of your video screen."

He allowed everyone a few minutes to open the prepared material, giving him time to steady his nerves. When it appeared everyone had opened the documents, Dale cleared his throat and nodded. "Ready?"

There were numerous "yeses."

"My document's blank," a jowl-faced man in his mid-fifties said.

"Oliver, are you clicking the info tab?" Dale asked.

"Oh, wait a minute." Oliver Banks peered over his glasses and leaned forward. The large screen magnified the scowl on his face. "Yes, here we go. I've got it now."

Dale forced himself to stay calm and took a seat. "Great, then we'll get started. As most of you know or have read by now, we've been having trouble with the Washington Heights development proj—"

"Yes, and it's time to shut that woman up." Oliver Banks banged a fist on the table. "You know what you need to do? You need to dig up some dirt on her. Everyone's hiding something."

"Hold that thought." Dale addressed him with as much deference as he could muster. But he despised the man for so many reasons, it was difficult not to clench his jaw when he spoke.

Oliver had been a constant source of consternation for his father and the lone vote against Dale taking over as CEO. He closed his eyes and blew out a breath through his nose. "At this point, the tide of public opinion is against us."

"And it's hurting our stock price, for goodness sakes." Banks' words came out in a growl. "We need to do something."

Dale clenched his fists beneath the table. "That's exactly why I called this meeting. We could break ground, begin building, and ignore the press and the protests, but I think it will hurt us in the long run. We risk losing money if no one wants to rent the apartments or retail space. It will further tarnish a reputation we've only recently begun to repair. And we stand the chance of losing future contracts. I've already received calls from clients and suppliers wondering what's going on."

"Can you blame them?" Imogene Carter, a redheaded woman in her forties, asked. "If I were them, I'd be worried, too."

Several members voiced their agreement.

"Exactly why we need to get out in front of this." Dale put his forearms on the table and leaned forward. "And by that, I mean we need to think not solely about our company, but what types of projects this company will need to create to regain the respect we once had when my father was running things." He paused, taking a sip of water to slow his heart rate and gauge the board members' reactions.

Imogene Carter, and board member Phillip Grange, a sixty-ish-looking man with a square jaw, slowly nodded.

Their agreement was enough of a signal for him to continue. "Look, we all know Wall Street lost confidence in Forester Industries when my father died." Dale cleared his throat. "Admittedly, my first two projects as CEO didn't go well, and…well…afterwards, we lost some bids. But as you can see, the chart on the second page of the proposal shows profits are on an upswing." He tapped his finger on the table several times to emphasize the point. "And I believe this project will go a long way in gaining back the credibility Forester Industries had with Charles Forester at the helm—translating into more projects, profits, and a higher stock price."

At the mention of his father, more board members nodded.

Dale sensed the momentum was with him, so he plowed ahead, jumping into the full presentation. For the next forty-five minutes, he took the board through his carefully laid-out plan. The pluses and the minuses were discussed, as well as the financial implications.

Questions about profits against any potential losses when making significant changes to an existing development plan were answered. Dale showed how the pros outweighed the cons, and the rise in goodwill could translate to an increase in the company stock price. Exhilarated at the end of his presentation, Dale left the room while the board voted.

The revised plan was passed by a vote of eleven to

one, the scowling Banks the lone dissenter. Dale now had the go-ahead to put his vision into action.

When the video screen went dark and the conference room cleared, a beaming Candace Forester hugged her son. “I’m so proud of you.”

Dale stepped back and loosened his tie. “I almost feel like that was the easy part.”

Candace tilted her head and pulled her brows together. “How so, dear?”

“Well, I still have to get Sylvia Ramirez’s support, and she might be a lot tougher than Oliver.”

Chapter 7

Sylvia and Randi arrived at the hospital, hoping to speak with Miguel's doctor for an update on his release. He'd suffered a broken arm, three fractured ribs, and a concussion. Thankfully, the tests showed no internal injuries.

Relieved to see Miguel awake, alert, and eating a bowl of vanilla ice cream, Sylvia took in a breath and relaxed her shoulders. "You gave us a scare."

"I don't know what happened. One minute I was standing on top of the ladder looking for the damn leak; the next thing I knew, I was here." Miguel shook his head.

"You fell. That's what happened," Sylvia said.

"Yeah, and on the way down, you crashed into stacks of old desks and chairs," Randi said. "Graceful, very graceful." She winked.

"Good morning, Mr. Cortez," came a greeting from the doorway. "I'm Rick, your day nurse."

Randi and Sylvia turned to find an athletic-looking man in blue scrubs pushing a computer cart into the room and positioning it next to Miguel's bed.

Walking to the counter, he pulled out two sterile plastic gloves from a box hanging on the wall and put them on. "I'm afraid we're gonna need a little privacy." Rick gestured toward Miguel while closing the curtains surrounding the bed.

"Oh, sure," Randi said. "Miguel, we'll be right outside."

As they waited in the hall, Sylvia leaned against the wall, unconsciously tapping her foot on the floor and making mental notes of strategies to keep the pressure on Forester Industries. She checked the time on her phone and huffed; the nurse took longer than expected. She could be doing a million things besides holding up this wall. "Hey, why don't you wait here? I'll make myself useful and head to the administration office to find out about his bill."

"That oughta be fun." Randi snorted.

"Yeah, loads. Can't wait." Sylvia waved and marched down the hall toward the elevators, pressed the button, and tapped her foot as the LED readout progressed from L to 5. When the doors finally opened, Sylvia's impatience nearly had her running into Carmen and Luís from the restaurant. "Oh! Sorry, guys."

"*Hola, mija.*" Carmen's large frame engulfed Sylvia in a hug. "How's he doing today?"

"His body is badly bruised, but, thank God, he suffered no internal injuries," Sylvia said.

Carmen made the sign of the cross. "*Gracias a Dios.*"

"Thank goodness for you," Sylvia said. "If you hadn't agreed to care for him while he heals, I'm not sure what we would have done. My apartment's the size of a tuna fish can."

Luís laughed. "Don't worry. He's like family."

Sylvia smiled. During yesterday's vigil, she discovered Miguel had become close to Luís and Carmen. In addition to going to culinary school at night, he'd begun apprenticing in the kitchen at their restaurant on the weekends. Carmen and Luís said it made sense to look after him, especially since their only son was away at college. They agreed it would be nice to have a full apartment again.

"Is he up?" Carmen asked.

"Yeah, but the nurse is in his room. He might be done now. I'm about to head over to the administration office. I'll be back in a few minutes."

They embraced once more.

Sylvia took the elevator to the lobby. She spent the next forty minutes at the hospital administrator's window haggling over Miguel's charges. In just two nights, the total was already in the thousands, and he had no health insurance. A quick glance at the bill showed they were charging a couple of hundred dollars for a few aspirins. "Seriously?" Sylvia pointed to the offending line. "Why didn't they ask me? I could've picked up a bottle of aspirin at the drugstore for less than five bucks."

The woman behind the glass gave a sympathetic smile and a non-committal shrug.

Her bureaucratic indifference made Sylvia's pulse race, and the pressure behind her eyes signaled the onset of a pounding headache. "Well, I'll let my attorney have a look at this. I can assure you, we'll be scrutinizing every line." Sylvia turned and walked away.

Arriving in the waiting area, she took a seat. With a copy of the hospital bill in one hand and her phone pressed to her ear with the other, she called the Legal Aid office where her parents had once worked. After explaining the situation to the receptionist, she was put on hold for the next available lawyer.

Humming along to the muzak, she leaned back in the chair, crossed her legs, and waited. When the third rotation of the same five songs began to play, Sylvia sighed. She stood, stretched, and checked the wall clock above the admittance desk. Tired of waiting, she pulled the phone away from her ear, about to swipe off the call.

"Hello, this is Jeremy Carona. How can I help you?"

The disembodied voice interrupted her mid-swipe, and Sylvia fumbled with the phone as she pulled it back to her ear. "Hello? Hello?"

"Yes, hello. This is Jeremy. Am I speaking with, ah, Sylvia Ramirez?"

"That's me." Pulling the straps of her purse over her shoulder, she moved a few feet away from the crowded waiting room. "The man who works for our community center was in an accident—"

"The Washington Heights Community Center? I saw it on the news. Tell me what happened to the custodian. Is he okay?"

"Yes, thank goodness. But he's been in the hospital for two days, and I need to discuss his bill—" The hospital's entrance doors slid open, and Sylvia stopped speaking mid-explanation.

As the hot air whooshed inside, so did Dale Forester.

Slack-jawed, Sylvia squinted, not believing her eyes. *What in the world is he doing here? Something's up.* "Uh…Jeremy, I'll have to get back to you." Ending the call, she stuffed her phone and the hospital bill into her purse.

Dale must have just alighted from his air-conditioned chauffeured ride because it was a million degrees out, and he looked perfect. Not a bead of perspiration sullied his upper lip, and his tailored suit draped his long, lean body in all the right places. She wanted to smack herself for having such a thought. *Girl, focus.* She pulled back her shoulders and mentally regrouped. She had to assume the only reason Dale Forester had come here was to do battle, so she needed to put up her shields and fire the first salvo. "What are *you* doing here?"

"Hello to you, too," Dale said. "How's Miguel?"

"You know him?"

"We, uh, ran into each other at the center the day I came to see you."

"Ahhh," Sylvia said.

"When do the doctors think he'll be able to go home?"

"Tomorrow." Sylvia's tone was guarded. She couldn't imagine what Dale was doing here. Before she could wrap her mind around that puzzle, she spied Randi coming around the corner.

Randi stopped a few feet behind Dale, pointing furiously at his back, mouthing the words, *Oh. My. God. Oh. My. God.*

Sylvia gave an almost imperceptible shake of her head, hoping Randi would notice and make herself scarce. Although she backed up another few feet, it was apparent Randi wasn't going anywhere; she intended to stay and listen unnoticed. Sylvia shifted her gaze from Randi, putting her attention back on Dale. "So, what really brings you here?"

Dale stepped closer. "I wanted to find out how Miguel was doing."

Sylvia furrowed her brow. “You could have called the hospital to find out.”

“Yes, I could have, but then I wouldn’t have run into you.”

“Me? How’d you know I’d be here?”

“Oh, come on, it wasn’t difficult to find you. You’ve been on the news for the last two days, holding a vigil for Miguel.” Dale gave a slight shrug. “So, naturally, it stood to reason you’d be here today—”

“Did you come all this way for the sole purpose of insulting me?” Sylvia said.

Dale put up a hand. “Sorry, that came out wrong. What I meant was, I hoped you’d be here. Once again, I’d like to propose we work together.”

From the corner of her eye, Sylvia saw Randi jump up and down, fist-bumping in the air and silently screaming, *Yes! Yes!*

Sylvia shook her head.

“Is that a no?” Dale asked.

“No.” Sylvia rushed to answer, glancing past him to glare at her best friend.

Randi had now struck a prayerful pose.

She had to force herself to ignore Randi and keep her attention on the conversation with Dale. “I mean, no, it’s not a no. Considering the recent events, it’s probably…I don’t know…worth exploring…you know, the possibility of, maybe…joining forces.” It killed her to have to ask this man for help. But she’d just seen Miguel’s hospital bill and needed some good news.

“I’m pleased to hear it.” Dale’s phone buzzed, and he held up an index finger. “Excuse me.” Pulling out his phone, he checked the screen. “I’m awfully sorry, but I have to take this.”

Sylvia gave a glassy stare. *Yeah, sure, whatever, Mr. Important.*

"Hi, can you hold on for one moment?" Dale said into his phone, then looked at Sylvia. "How about dinner tonight?"

Sylvia did a double take. "Me?"

"Yes." He was smiling now. "I'd like to tell you what I have in mind, and the sooner, the better. Besides, I can think of better places to have a conversation than a hospital waiting room."

In her peripheral vision, she saw Randi waving her arms like ground control on an airport tarmac, mouthing the words, *say yes.*

Sylvia froze. Dinner with Dale Forester wasn't the best idea she'd ever heard of, but she was running out of options. If she thought about it, she was backed into a corner with no window or door for an exit. "Okay. Dinner." Her words came out in a rush.

Dale grinned. "Great. My assistant, Peter, will text you the time and address of the restaurant, if that works for you."

Sylvia nodded. "Sure."

Dale gave her a small smile.

She watched him turn and walk toward the exit, put his phone back to his ear, and continue with whatever meaningful conversation he was bound to be having.

As soon as he was out the door, Randi ran to her and grabbed both her hands. "Gur-r-l-l-l-l-l, this is the best news we've had all week."

"I don't know." Sylvia bit her lower lip. "What could he possibly offer? He's already got the development deal from the city."

Randi cocked her head. "He could say he's

building a new center. Or, at the very least, he fully funds the college scholarship program."

"Ha! You are *so* dreaming."

"It could happen." Randi gave Sylvia a light punch on her arm. "Remember, he's got a public relations problem. We're the ones getting all the media attention." She took a step closer, putting her face inches from Sylvia's. "Hey, where's the woman I know? The one with the positive attitude? Huh?"

Sylvia gave a weak smile. "I've had a few setbacks of late. Or hadn't you noticed?"

"But this could be the break we need."

"Yeah, but this goes against everything I believe. He's a Forester, for pity's sakes. Have you forgotten?" Sylvia clenched the strap of her purse. The acid in her stomach churned as the day presented her with one unwanted situation after the next.

Randi put her hands on her hips. "Listen, you are perilously close to becoming an overplayed song. You have to at least hear him out for the sake of the center." She tugged on Sylvia's hands. "You need to stop being so righteous and closed-minded. It's not an attractive look. And in case you don't know, help doesn't have to hurt. Just saying."

Sylvia closed her eyes. "Okay." She huffed out a breath. "Fine. But only for the sake of the center."

"That's what I'm talking about!" Randi grinned and lifted her palm overhead, ready to give Sylvia a high five.

Sylvia didn't respond.

Randi's eyes widened. "What? You gonna leave me hangin' here?"

Sylvia gave Randi a half-smile and reluctantly

lifted her hand.

They slapped palms.

Randi bounced on the balls of her feet. "Okay, this is good. This is real good."

Despite Randi's enthusiasm, Sylvia had doubts. She wondered if having dinner with the man who had been her arch-rival was a smart move.

Chapter 8

Several hours later, Sylvia checked her lipstick in the mirror and then turned to survey her studio apartment. It looked like a crime scene. She'd spent the last two hours combing through her clothes for something to wear, and now, the entire contents of her closet covered every available surface. She'd finally settled on a pair of black, high-waisted, wide-bottom pants and a black sleeveless top with white piping. The effect was dramatic.

"Girl, stop checking yourself in the mirror." Randi strode in from the kitchen area, drinking a can of soda. "I already told you, it's a killer look. Besides, this is a business dinner." She raised one brow. "Emphasis on the word *biz-ness*."

"Oh, please. I know this isn't a social get-together." Sylvia faced the mirror, puckered her lips, and applied more gloss with her pinkie. "I want one thing from him and one thing only."

"Exactly. Be strong, and don't come back until he guarantees you a new center."

Sylvia huffed. "I'll be sure to keep that in mind. If he doesn't come through with an offer, I'll stab him to death with my salad fork."

"I know you think you're being funny, but I wouldn't put it past you. So don't overreact if he says something stupid. And please, *try* to be nice."

Sylvia turned to face Randi. Her insides felt like jelly. "Okay, coach, wanna ease up? I'm already nervous."

"Why would you be nervous?"

Sylvia put her index finger to her chin and tilted her head. "Hmm. Let me think. Could it be the entire future of The Heights just might be decided by this little dinner tonight?"

Randi put her soda on the coffee table and took several steps toward Sylvia until they were inches apart. "You are the strongest woman I know. You've made miracles happen. You can, and you will do this. I have faith in you." She squeezed Sylvia's shoulder. "Now stop whining and bring back the goods."

Sylvia's phone buzzed. She picked it up and glanced at the screen. "My car's here." She kissed Randi on the cheek. "Lock up when you leave."

"You better text me when you get home. I want details," Randi said.

"I'll take notes just for you." Sylvia snorted and walked out the door. Holding on to the handrail, she began the trek down the five flights of stairs. With each step, her leg muscles twitched and gyrated like contestants in a *merengue* dance-off.

Dressing up and heading out for an expensive meal reminded her of being with her ex. She bit her lower lip, stopped mid-step, and squeezed her eyes shut. Why did she think about Julian? Tall, broad-shouldered, sandy-haired Julian. Sylvia sighed deeply, opened her eyes, and continued down the stairs. But she couldn't shake his image. How had she gotten that relationship so wrong?

They'd been introduced through a mutual friend,

and instant electricity surged between them from the first hello. For the next six months, they were inseparable. If one searched the dictionary for the definition of "whirlwind romance," they'd find a cuddly selfie of Julian and Sylvia, illustrating the point.

When he invited her to meet his parents, she was thrilled. It signaled they were moving on to the next step. To something more permanent. More forever. At least, she hoped. But the evening turned out to be nothing like the casual meet-and-greet dinner Julian promised.

Ushered into the family home by a butler, Sylvia bit her tongue to stop the word "wow" from escaping her lips. His parents' reception was lukewarm, as if she were a door-to-door salesperson who'd stumbled into the wrong neighborhood. The conversation during cocktail hour was stilted but mercifully cut short when the butler announced dinner was served ten minutes into the first martini.

The five-course meal had been the most agonizing portion of the evening. His parents grilled her between plates of lobster, Kobe beef, imported truffles, and a twenty-year-old Chateau something-or-other. No question had been off-limits. They quizzed her about her family, friends, and work. They'd practically demanded to see her résumé.

The strained smiles on their faces as she thanked them for dinner and said goodnight could only be interpreted as disapproval.

The next day, Julian confessed his parents threatened to cut him off if he pursued the relationship.

She couldn't believe what he was saying. Her parents could only afford the necessities, but while growing up, Sylvia never felt deprived.

Julian, however, hadn't known a day without the comfort and privilege of extraordinary wealth. Choosing money over her had been her biggest heartbreak. In an instant, their relationship went from I-can't-live-without-you to Sylvia *who*? And it had taken all of two days for Julian to ghost her completely.

From then on, she vowed she could work with people who had money and raise funds from the wealthy, but she would never become personally involved again. People with unlimited financial resources couldn't be trusted. She'd learned that lesson the hard way.

So why was she in such a literal tizzy over this dinner? She hated herself for reacting to Dale's charm. She meant to hate him and everything he stood for. Instead, butterflies danced in her stomach when she thought about his dark hair falling over one eye when he'd turned, smiled, and asked her to dinner. *Stop it. You're being ridiculous.*

Sliding into the waiting taxi, she took a deep breath and sat back against the faux leather. As the car pulled away from the curb, she tried to collect her thoughts. "Would you mind taking the highway?" Sylvia called to the driver as they drove west on 181st Street.

He looked in the rearview mirror and nodded.

The traffic was light, and the ride was smooth as they sailed down the West Side Highway. The setting sun reflecting off the glistening water of the Hudson River gave it an almost jeweled look. Sylvia smiled. What was there to be nervous about? She knew what she had to do, and she couldn't let nerves, or Dale's charming ways, distract her.

The restaurant, Le Jardin, was located on a tree-lined street. Tiny white lights sparkled at the entrance window. If she didn't know what she was looking for, she might have mistaken it for another multi-million-dollar brownstone on one of the most expensive parcels of real estate on Manhattan's Upper West Side. The moment she stepped out of the car, the restaurant's front door opened, and she faced a tall, stately man in an elegant double-breasted suit and a white boutonniere in his lapel.

"Good evening, Ms. Ramirez. I'm Mitchell, the maître d'. Mr. Forester is waiting in our terrace garden. If you will follow me, please."

That was odd. How did this man know her name? She could have been one of a dozen diners. Maybe it was just one more quirk of the rich. She stepped inside the small but elegant French eatery and silently gasped. Except for the wait staff, the restaurant was empty.

On her left stood a lone bartender polishing the already gleaming mahogany bar top. The room opened out to feature fifteen tables covered in white linen. Dozens of candles produced a warm glow, and the air was perfumed with the scent of roses. The entire setup made her nervous. Perspiration pooled at the small of her back. "Where is everyone?"

Instead of answering, the maître d' gave a slight bow. "Follow me."

She hesitated. Should she follow him? Or should she dig her three-inch heels into the hardwood floor and say, *Hold up, Mitch. What's going on?* Sylvia chose to remain silent. The situation intrigued her, but more importantly, she was on a mission to save the center. So, she continued in Mitchell's wake, walking past the beautifully set but empty tables.

They reached a wall of glass doors leading out to an impeccably manicured, candlelit garden. The maître d' slid open the door.

Seated at a table for two, Dale looked disarmingly handsome in a dark jacket and open-necked light blue shirt. He gave her a slow smile, rose, and stepped out from behind the table. "Hi, Sylvia."

She had to focus on her mission, not on how good he looked. "Hello."

Dale motioned for her to join him at the table.

Before crossing the threshold, she needed to rid herself of the uninvited troupe of circus acrobats who were now performing somersaults in the pit of her stomach. She shook her head. Agreeing to this dinner had been a mistake. If not for the low chant in the back of her mind—*Save the center. Save the center. Save the center*—she would have turned around. Instead, she gave a tight smile and continued toward the table.

Mitchell pulled out her chair, placed the napkin across her lap, and stepped away.

She kept her expression neutral, trying not to notice Dale examining her every move. Clasping her hands tightly beneath the table, she waited for him to speak first. To explain this little seduction.

"Would you care for water?" A tall, thin server appeared out of nowhere.

Sylvia looked up. "Yes, please." She kept her focus on the pour. When he stepped away, she reached for the water and drank deeply. She licked her lips and put down the glass. Only then did she realize it was empty.

"Would you care for more?" The server once again appeared at her side.

How does he move without making a sound? She nodded. Avoiding Dale's gaze, she concentrated on her water glass while her mind buzzed. What the heck was going on? Clearly, Dale had reserved the entire establishment for the evening. But why?

Sylvia quickly took in her surroundings. She had to give him credit. He had good taste. The restaurant had an old-world charm. White-washed brick walls formed the perimeter. Artfully placed ivy trailed down the center wall. All three were fronted by lilac bushes, creating a heady fragrance. Strung overhead were tiny white lights, giving the feel of an enchanted garden.

"I'm glad you could make it." Dale smiled, then gave an almost imperceptible nod.

The server instantly appeared once more.

This was freaking her out; *how could anyone move with such stealth*?

The server lifted a bottle from the ice bucket. "Champagne?"

She only had to look up.

He began to pour.

Mentally, her jaw dropped. *Champagne?*

When both flutes were filled, the server silently glided away.

Dale lifted his glass. "A toast."

Sylvia clenched her fingers around her glass. She had just about enough. "What's the occasion?"

Dale gave a toothy smile. "To the future of a promising working relationship." He clinked his glass against hers and took a drink.

Sylvia put down her glass. "Thanks for the atmosphere, but I thought this was business."

Dale's brow wrinkled. "It is."

“Really? So why did you buy out the entire restaurant for a business meeting?” The edge in Sylvia’s voice was sharp. *Oh, no, no, no, no, no!* She could hear Randi’s voice, *don’t ruin it. You only need to like him. Not LIKE-like him.*

Sylvia took in a breath. Randi was right. She’d have to push aside her annoyance and make this dinner work. It was a big ask. After all, no one had ever accused her of being charming.

Chapter 9

Dale glanced at the champagne bottle in the ice bucket and thought about how to answer Sylvia's question. Of course, she was right. He wouldn't have bought out an entire restaurant for a business meeting. If he were being honest, he supposed he'd been trying to impress her. And if she'd been anyone else, it would have worked. But she wasn't like anyone he'd ever met, worked with, or dated. His usual go-to moves seem to have no sway. "You know what? You're right. And I apologize if this upsets you."

"I wouldn't say I was upset. I simply don't understand why you went to all this trouble."

Despite her words, her arched eyebrow seemed to announce her displeasure. He cleared his throat. "I tend to get recognized wherever I go, and I wanted us to discuss our business without any interruptions."

Sylvia scoffed. "Well, if that's all you wanted, you could have asked me for recommendations. I know dozens of places that serve terrific food, and no one would have known who you were or cared."

Dale refused to acknowledge the dig. Instead, he took a sip of champagne. "What makes you such an expert on restaurants in the city?"

"My father taught me." At the mention of her father, her shoulders dropped, and the muscles in her face relaxed.

"How so?" he asked.

Sylvia shook her head. "It's not important."

"Oh, come on. Don't stop yourself now."

"No. It's a long story." Sylvia waved her hand. "Forget I said anything." Crossing her arms, she sat back.

"Sorry. I can't." Dale put down his champagne flute and fixed his gaze on her. "You've piqued my curiosity. Come on. I'd really like to hear it." To his surprise, he found he did want to hear her story.

"Okay. You asked for it." Sylvia put her face in her hands. "I can't believe I'm about to tell you this." She looked up and smiled.

Her eyes seemed to sparkle in the candlelight, and Dale thought she should smile more often.

"When I was twelve," Sylvia said, "we lived next door to a wonderful woman named Mrs. Warchovsky, the unofficial babysitter for the neighborhood kids. We played outside, and she kept an eye on us from her second-floor window. Mrs. W was a widow. Her children were grown and scattered across the country." Sylvia paused.

Dale stared at the crease in her brow. "Something wrong?"

"No. I was thinking she must have been lonely because when she wasn't looking out her window, she kept herself busy by cooking. Some days you could smell the onions frying at six in the morning." Sylvia fanned her nose.

Dale laughed. He leaned forward, placing his chin in his hand.

"Every week, she would make big batches of Polish dishes, put them in containers, and hand them to all the neighbors."

"She sounds interesting."

"Oh, believe me, she was interesting and then some. She knew what was happening on the block before it happened." Sylvia chuckled. "Anyway, one night, my parents came home from work late and were too tired to cook. So, my mother took a batch of Mrs. W's pierogies from the freezer, heated them, and served them for dinner. I'd never heard of pierogies. I refused to eat them." Sylvia cleared her throat. "Actually, I threw a tantrum. My father calmly sat through my hysterics, but I think he was more disappointed than upset by my hell-child behavior."

"Oh, so being difficult isn't a new trait. Sounds like you've been perfecting that particular characteristic for a while." Dale smirked but inwardly was delighted by the story.

"Ha, ha. Very funny." Sylvia smirked back.

Dale put up both hands and grinned. "Sorry. I was trying to be funny. Forget I said anything. I want to hear how this story ends."

Sylvia remained silent, although one corner of her mouth was raised in a semi-smile.

"Oh, come on," Dale said. "I was joking. Seriously, please continue."

"All right. But only because you asked nicely." Sylvia took in a deep breath. "Before they sent me to bed without supper, my father told me I had no sense of adventure. And right then and there, he decided I needed a culinary education." She paused, twisting her water glass.

In the candlelight, Dale noticed a blush creep up her neck, slowly making its way up her cheeks. Could it be she was embarrassed? A surprising occurrence coming from the likes of Sylvia Ramirez. "Is anything wrong?"

"No, nothing." She bit her lower lip. "I don't usually like to talk about my personal life with people I don't know."

"Well, you're too deep into the story to stop now." Dale cocked his head and smiled. A warm feeling filled his chest. He was entranced. "Please. I'd like to hear all about your culinary education."

"Nah, that's okay. There's really…well, that's all. Really." She folded her hands on the table.

Dale couldn't leave it. "Come on. You've got me hooked. I need to know how this story ends."

Sylvia took in a long breath, and her face softened. "Well, that's what was so special about my father. What could have been an awful night ending in tears and recriminations turned out to be the beginning of one of my family's greatest traditions. On the first Sunday of every month, after church, instead of a family meal at home, we would eat in a new country by exploring the different neighborhoods in New York City."

Dale couldn't contain his smile. He could listen to her all night long. "That sounds fabulous."

"Oh, it was. Every month was new cuisine—Chinese, Italian, Greek, Russian, Indian, Ethiopian, and German." Sylvia ticked off the list on her fingers. "From delis to family-owned restaurants, holes-in-the-wall to street vendor carts. You name it, and we ate it."

The idea charmed him. Dale put his elbows on the table and steepled his hands beneath his chin. "You surprise me. I bet you know more about where to eat in this town than I do."

She smiled. "Well, I definitely know the places off the beaten path. You know, authentic cuisine not written about in culinary reviews"—she pointed her finger in his direction—"but I bet the food could rival some of the five-star restaurants you frequent."

"You'll have to take me to one of your favorites sometime."

"That's a date." Sylvia's eyes widened. "I didn't mean a *date* date."

Dale chuckled. "I know what you meant. Well, since we're on the topic of food, are you ready to order?" He motioned for the server.

The man sailed silently up to the table and quickly presented them with menus.

Dale studied Sylvia as she reviewed the choices. Her face glowed in the candlelight. Her brown eyes sparkled. *She is beautiful.*

"Have you decided, sir?" the server asked.

Dale nodded toward Sylvia. "After you."

"I'll have the chicken *piccata*. Thanks."

"And to start?" The server asked.

"Ummm…the radicchio salad."

"And for you, sir?"

Dale ordered what he usually enjoyed whenever he came to this restaurant—the escargot and lobster with cauliflower and truffle.

Wordlessly, the server took the menus and drifted away.

Dale had planned to jump into the new proposal as soon as they ordered, but getting to know her held more interest. He cleared his throat, searching for something to say to keep this informal conversation going. "My mother is a big admirer." As soon as the words were out, he wanted to pull them back. He sounded so lame.

"Really? Your mother? I've never even met her."

"You haven't." Dale paused. How could Sylvia know Candace Forester was a big part of his life? She'd helped his father build Forester Industries and was now an important member of the Forester Board of Directors. "But since we're going to be in business together, she looked you up on-line."

"Seriously?" Sylvia narrowed her gaze.

"Don't act so surprised. You mean to tell me you've never checked out another person's social media footprint?"

Sylvia shook her head. "You know you can't believe everything you read. People post stuff on social media, and everyone assumes it's the truth, without further investigation."

He hadn't thought their conversation would lead to this subject. But here they were, with no choice but for him to plow on, despite the uncomfortable niggle at the back of his neck. "You're right, and if anyone knows that, it's me. I've had more total fabrications written about me than I care to remember." Dale raised both eyebrows. "I'm talking about doctored photos to make it look like I'm sunning on a beach I've never even heard of, let alone visited."

Sylvia gave him what looked like a sympathetic grin, but he knew it was meant to be a smirk. She seemed to be good at smirking. "I know what you're thinking,"—he pointed a finger—"yes, there were stories that contained a grain of truth. But really, you must believe me, a lot of the stuff was made up of thin air."

Sylvia put up one hand like a traffic cop. "I'm not judging."

"A little, yes, you are." Dale couldn't help but smile.

Sylvia laughed. "Okay, yes. There was a cartoon bubble over my head, and it was filled with judgment."

Her laugh was light, almost musical, and to Dale's surprise, everything about Sylvia captivated him. He wanted to respond and be witty, but he found himself searching for words that wouldn't come.

"Excuse me."

To Dale's relief, the server interrupted the lull in the conversation and served the appetizers.

They ate in silence for a few moments.

"Anyway, you have nothing to worry about," Dale continued, finally finding his voice. "The Internet thinks you're terrific. A search on you yields nothing but one amazing story after the next."

Sylvia arched a brow and pointed her fork. "Really? You sure about that?"

Dale coughed and wiped the corner of his mouth with his napkin.

"Are you going to avoid the elephant sitting right at this table?" Sylvia asked.

Dale looked at his plate, pulled a garlic-soaked snail out of its shell, and popped it into his mouth. "I hadn't planned on bringing it up."

"Then I will." She gave a one shoulder shrug. "I'm a troublemaker. I like to make trouble."

"I wouldn't call it trouble." Dale surveyed the lights in the garden, hoping if he stalled long enough, he'd figure out what to say. He wanted to avoid an argument at all costs. "I think you're…determined. I think you fight for what you believe in, even though sometimes what you believe in isn't always right."

"I beg your pardon." Sylvia put down her fork with enough force the water glasses vibrated. "There isn't a cause I've stood for, marched with, or spoken about that wasn't on the side of right."

"Depends on whose side you're on."

"Listen, Mr. Forester—"

Dale put up his hand. "Let's not fight. We're on the same side now."

The right side of her mouth lifted and she interlaced her fingers on the table. "How so?"

"That's what this dinner is all about."

"You mean you weren't about to mention I was arrested two years ago for protesting the West Side Highway development?"

Dale laughed, a deep, hearty laugh.

"I'm glad you find my incarceration funny. I wasn't amused." Sylvia pursed her lips.

"Sorry. I wasn't laughing at you. And the term 'incarceration' is a bit much. You spent one night in jail."

"Easy for you to say." Sylvia paused closing her eyes in an attempt to hold back her frustration. "Have you ever been put behind bars for a cause you believed in? Even for a day?"

Dale didn't respond.

"That's what I thought," Sylvia huffed.

"Look, what happened was wrong. No one should ever be arrested for peaceful assembly." Dale tapped his index finger on the table to make a point.

Sylvia looked as if she were about to speak but stopped and closed her eyes. She remained silent for several seconds, and her shoulders seemed to drop a few inches. Then she reached across the table and put her hand over his. “Thanks. Really. Thanks for saying that.”

Dale wasn’t prepared for what he felt from her touch. It was entirely new. Something he’d not experienced with any other woman. *Dangerous territory.* They were going to be in business together. Any other type of “together” was off the table. He quickly took his hand away. “So, let’s talk about a new community center.”

Chapter 10

Three days later, Dale slipped into the buttery leather seat of the Forester corporate jet and checked his phone for missed calls or texts. He sighed—still no message from Sylvia. Rational or not, he had hoped she would call or at least signal her excitement with a text. After all, Forester Industries was going to great expense to create a new community center in the Washington Heights Development. A simple smile emoji would have been sufficient. But to his surprise, he'd heard nothing since their dinner together. He'd never been so thoroughly ignored.

"Mr. Forester, we're about to take off. Please fasten your seat belt."

"Thanks, Margaret." Dale smiled at the tall woman with gentle eyes and laugh lines around her mouth. She'd been the flight attendant on the Forester Industries' jet for half his lifetime.

"Once we're in the air, can I bring you anything?"

"Iced coffee, black, please." Dale tossed his phone onto the seat next to him, fastened his seat belt, and let out one, long sigh. Who was he kidding? The development, while important, wasn't his main concern at the moment. He simply wanted to hear from Sylvia…about anything.

The thought caught him by surprise. He never expected their relationship to be anything more than cordial, considering up to now, Sylvia had worked hard to try to ruin Forester Industries. But their evening at Le Jardin changed everything. Her usual defensive hard edges had melted away, and he found himself leaning in, wanting to get to know this woman.

As the evening flew by, she revealed her love for the people in her neighborhood and her willingness to help others. He admired her passion and now understood why she fought so hard. Unlike any woman he'd ever known, Sylvia intrigued him. Dale blew out a breath and shifted in his seat. What in the name of self-preservation was he doing? These constant thoughts of Sylvia Ramirez were putting him on dangerous ground. Quicksand would provide more emotional purchase.

Running his hands through his hair, he sat up, looked at his briefcase, checked his watch, and shook his head in an attempt to get into the present. The meeting at the Buffalo site would start in less than two hours, and he had to get a grip. The reports from the field weren't adding up. The last thing he needed was trouble on this project. He folded up his shirt sleeves, took several folders from his briefcase, and began reading.

An hour and a half later, as the jet descended into the Buffalo airport, his phone chimed. Snatching it from underneath the stack of work papers, he answered without looking. "Hello?"

"Hello, darling."

Dale slumped against his seat. "Oh, hello, Mother. We're about to land, and I'm just finishing up a report. Is everything all right?"

"Yes, of course. But I want to remind you the Silverlight Charity Ball is in two months, and the

Chairman called to tell me they haven't received your RSVP."

Dale didn't respond because he didn't know what to say. He rested his phone between his shoulder and ear and stuffed the reports into his briefcase.

"Your silence tells me everything, dear. I knew you'd forgotten. You have two assistants, a smartphone, and a tablet. Did you purposefully not put this in your calendar?"

Dale loved his mother, but there were times when it was difficult not to be annoyed. This was one of those instances. He closed his eyes, pinched the bridge of his nose, and remained silent for a moment to avoid sounding harsh when he spoke.

"Hello? Did I lose you?"

"Nope. I'm here." Dale huffed under his breath. "Couldn't I write a check and be done with it? Do I need to get dressed up and spend two or three hours in small talk with people I don't care about when I'll end up giving money anyway? What is the point? It seems like a wasted evening." He snapped shut his briefcase.

"Might I remind you we've had a public relations issue of late, and the smart move is to put on your best face and show the rest of the world you're doing fine? There's no better place to do that than at the Silverlight Ball. It's the event of the season."

Dale let out an enormous sigh. He felt like a ten-year-old being sent to clean up his room. "Okay, Mother. I'll be there."

"And bring a date."

Dale rested his forehead in the palm of his hand. "I'm not dating anyone. Who would I bring?"

"Again, you have a smartphone and a tablet. I'm

sure there must be any number of young women you could ask. That's it for now. Talk soon."

Dale pulled the phone from his ear and stared at it. She'd hung up. He shook his head and leaned back in his seat as the plane's landing wheels hit the tarmac. Irritation prickled at the back of his neck. "Bring a date," Dale murmured under his breath and frowned. He couldn't imagine who he'd bring. Mentally flipping through his contacts, Dale couldn't keep a slow smile from spreading across his face, and as an idea formed he chuckled. If his mother thought they needed a public relations lift, maybe he'd asked Sylvia Ramirez. Appearing together as a couple might help put the negative gossip to rest. Dale shifted in his seat. Could he dare ask her? Would she even say yes?

****

One week later, Dale was back in New York City, sitting in the mayor's office, drumming his fingers on the portfolio in his lap.

Mayor Simms sat across from him, occupied with papers on his desk.

The only sound came from the small window air-conditioner, chugging and gurgling loudly, barely keeping pace with the rising temperature in the room. He tugged at his shirt collar, stifling the urge to loosen his tie. Instead, he crossed his legs, glanced at his watch, and blew out a breath.

"She's late." The mayor barely raised his gaze from the work in front of him.

Shrugging in response, Dale continued drumming his fingers on the portfolio. *What was keeping her?* He was CEO of one of the country's largest real estate firms. No one kept him waiting. He checked his watch again. It had been over a week since their non-date, and Sylvia still hadn't reached out. It irritated him to the point of distraction. On the flight home from the Buffalo site, he'd decided his preoccupation with her had to stop. From now on, he'd keep her at arm's length. He'd think about rocks if he had to, anything to get her out of his mind. He knew it was the best course of action for him and this project.

Dale recrossed his legs and absently jiggled his foot. *Where is she?* He was about to let out another annoyed breath when the intercom on the mayor's desk buzzed.

"Ms. Ramirez is here, sir," announced the mayor's assistant.

No sooner had the words floated out of the speaker than Sylvia breezed into the room.

Dale stood and stared. She was stunning. Her hair was pushed up high in a messy bun, jeans framed every curve, and high-heeled sandals gave her just enough height.

"Sorry. The subway." Sylvia shrugged, directing the comment toward the mayor as if he oversaw every train in the New York City Metropolitan Transit System. She gave Dale a quick smile and sat in the chair next to his.

She was close enough for him to breathe in her lemon scent. His knees wobbled, and his resolve to keep her at arm's length crumbled like the last hard cookie at the bottom of the bag.

"Let's get started." Mayor Simms gestured toward Dale.

"Thank you." Dale sat and fished out several folders from his portfolio, spreading them across the mayor's large oak desk. He cleared his throat. "Here are the original plans for the development." Dale pointed to a set of blueprints on his right. "Now, these"—he pulled out a second set of blueprints and laid them over the first—"are the revisions we'd like to make. My chief architect has arranged a meeting with the Washington Heights Planning Board to review, and hopefully accept, these new plans."

Perspiration dripped down Dale's back, and it wasn't only because of the warm temperature in the room. Being this close to Sylvia made him nervous. He wanted to impress her. He wanted her to like the revisions he'd made to the development. He wanted to make her happy with the new community center. The only other person he'd ever wished to please had been his father. Glancing from the corner of his eye, he tried to gauge Sylvia's reaction.

She sat without moving. Her facial expression remained neutral.

Dale couldn't read her body language.

"Go on," the mayor said.

Dale hadn't realized he'd stopped talking and had been staring at Sylvia. "Sorry." He blinked several times to clear his head. "Forester Industries is also working with the City Planning Board to determine how many apartments will be designated as affordable housing and who will be eligible to rent them. Right now, they're considering a lottery system."

"That's incredible." Sylvia uncrossed her arms and leaned forward, focusing on the new plans. A lock of hair fell across her face.

Dale had to stop himself from placing it back behind her ear. "We'll need your help with the new community center, Ms. Ramirez. No one knows the neighborhood and its people better than you do." He turned to face her. "To start, I'd like you to propose a list of exactly what the new center will need."

Sylvia picked up the blueprints and examined them.

"So, give us your thoughts, Ms. Ramirez?" The mayor leaned forward.

Sylvia didn't answer the question. Instead, she carefully placed the blueprints on the mayor's desk and sat back while her gaze lingered on the designs.

Dale checked his watch and forced himself to sit still, but the anticipation was too much, and he unconsciously chewed on the inside of his cheek, waiting for her to say something…anything.

Sylvia remained silent for several more moments before she rose from her chair and offered Dale her hand.

Halfway out of his seat, he held out his hand to shake on the new plans.

Sylvia threw her arms around his neck. Pressing her lips against his ear, she whispered, "Thank you."

Caught off guard, Dale spontaneously returned the hug. The warmth of her cheek, coupled with her citrusy scent, was intoxicating. Overwhelmed with the sudden urge to kiss her, he pulled away and ran a hand through his hair, trying to slow the intense beating of his heart. The heat rising to his face threatened to expose his feelings, so he looked down, feigning interest in the floor tile while hoping to regain his composure. After a moment, he took in a breath and looked up.

Sylvia stood with her hand over her heart. "I hardly know what to say. I've been fighting to be heard for so long. I mean, well, it's just…no one has ever asked me what I thought before."

"That was a major oversight." Dale's voice was soft, and he lowered his eyes.

"Honestly, I'm thrilled." Sylvia beamed. "This development will benefit so many."

"I'm happy to hear you say that. Keep in mind, there are still plenty of issues for you to discuss with my chief planner and architect. I'll arrange to have those meetings set up."

"And *I* want to make sure we have your complete buy-in." The mayor pointed to Sylvia. "We'll make a major announcement to the media next week, and we need to be on the same page. I don't want any demonstrations." Mayor Simms raised his eyebrows. "No surprises."

"Don't worry. This will be the first time I will address the media with good news." Sylvia clasped her hands together. "I am one hundred percent behind this project."

The mayor stood. "Okay, you two, I have a busy day. I'm sure you both can work out the details. Let's meet with the city council in a week, and we'll review what needs to be done. I'll have my assistant put it on the schedule and send out invites to everyone who needs to be present."

"Thank you, Mayor," Dale and Sylvia said in unison. They shook hands with the mayor and headed out the door, making their way toward the elevators.

Alone in the small space, Dale couldn't keep his gaze off Sylvia. As the ancient elevator car made its descent to street level, his grin widened, watching her bounce on the balls of her feet. Her excitement mirrored his, and an indescribable lightness seem to flow up from inside his chest and float through the top of his head, as if champagne bubbles were popping all around. With each pop, another doubt or worry evaporated. He hadn't felt this light or excited about anything in too long.

"This is remarkable." Sylvia fanned herself with a hand. "And just so we're clear, I'm really, really, really happy that you're doing this. It couldn't have been easy to get everyone to agree with this new direction."

He gave a half-laugh. "I'll admit, it took a bit of persuasion."

"Well, I appreciate it more than you know, but…." Sylvia took a breath as they stepped off the elevator. "I was thinking—"

"Already?" Dale raised an eyebrow.

"Yes." Sylvia gave a decisive nod. "I was thinking, now that we're moving forward with a new community center, I'd like to propose a few additions. Are you good with that?"

They continued talking as they walked down the many steps outside City Hall.

"Depends on what they are. We're still in the planning stages, so it's possible to make a few changes."

Sylvia grinned. "I'm happy to hear it because our kids need to be part of the twenty-first century, and to help them get there, we're going to need a room with lots of computers and high-speed internet. Most of these students don't have computers at home, and they'll need them to be competitive on their SATs."

Her energy seemed to build as she spoke, and Dale was mesmerized by the sheer aliveness in her face.

"You know, if I'm allowed to dream here"—Sylvia gave a coy smile—"having an indoor swimming pool and two gymnasiums would be great, and I've always thought we should have a greenhouse." Sylvia's eyes widened. "We could even create a community garden where the people in the neighborhood could grow their own produce and teach the kids how to start a garden from seeds."

"Whoa, hold on." Dale stopped and rubbed the back of his neck. "Those are great ideas. But we have a budget, and part of my job is to ensure we stick to it."

"And who do you think you're dealing with?" Sylvia patted his arm and continued down the steps. "Remember, I run a non-profit community center. I'm used to squeezing a nickel until the buffalo runs off the coin. And that's before I get into the dialing-for-dollars, fundraising mode."

With the firsthand knowledge that Sylvia Ramirez tended to get exactly what she wanted, Dale let out a laugh. They reached the sidewalk, where Dale's black SUV waited. He hesitated and turned before getting into the passenger seat. "Can I give you a lift?"

"Thanks." Sylvia shook her head. "I'm too excited to sit in a car. I want to walk off this excess energy and enjoy the beautiful day."

Dale agreed the day was glorious. The sunshine highlighted the rich auburn tones in her hair, and her face seemed to glow. She was stunning. "I'm happy that you're happy."

"You know"—Sylvia wagged a finger—"it just occurred to me that you're saving a neighborhood you've never actually visited."

Dale chuckled. "Of course, I've been there."

"No, you haven't."

"Wait, what are you saying? I was there a few weeks ago. You do remember our meeting in your office?" Dale held onto the opened car door, wondering what she was getting at.

Sylvia raised one eyebrow. "Oh, no. Let's be clear. Driving up in your air-conditioned, super-expensive luxury automobile, with its tinted windows rolled up, and then visiting an enclosed office for one half hour in no way qualifies as having seen The Heights."

Surprised she'd spoken that entire thought without losing her breath, he had no choice but to consider what she'd said. "Is that a challenge?"

Sylvia threw her head back with a laugh. "Absolutely."

Dale leaned forward. Was she flirting? Whatever it was, he couldn't stop staring. "So, what exactly are you proposing?"

"Cancel whatever appointments you have tomorrow." Sylvia smiled.

"Tomorrow's Saturday. I planned on catching up on paperwork in the office."

"Great. I'll pick you up outside your office at noon. Don't be late." She turned to walk away.

Dale held up a hand. "Wait, what will we be doing?"

Sylvia turned back to face him. "You'll find out." She grinned. "Oh, and dress casual."

Dale's gaze followed her as she walked away. Without a doubt, a flirty vibe had passed between them as evidenced by his accelerated heart rate and sweaty palms. *You're in trouble now, Forester.*

Chapter 11

Randi flung herself into Sylvia's overstuffed armchair and picked up her *café con leche* from the old-fashioned steamer trunk that doubled as an underwear drawer and coffee table. "Look, I'm super excited we're getting a new center. I am. I swear."

"I feel a *but* coming." Sylvia fanned herself with a hand. The temperature in her apartment was hotter than outside or maybe it was nerves.

"There's no but. It's just—I didn't expect you to get up close and personal with the guy. I mean, it was only a few days ago he was archenemy *numero uno*."

"He is not the enemy. Well, at least not anymore," Sylvia called out from inside her closet.

"Oh, so that's how you're gonna play it. If I remember correctly, *chica*, you're the one who couldn't stop telling me about how those Foresters couldn't be trusted. Shouldn't you be at least a little cautious? Like, take off the dark sunglasses and have a real look?"

"This is different." Sylvia stepped out of the closet, holding up a black short-sleeved shirt. "How does this look?"

"Why do you feel like you need a wardrobe check every time you see this guy?" Randi gave Sylvia a sideways glance. "It's like I'm watching *Pretty Woman* on a loop. What's up with that? You aren't dressing to impress, right? Cause this is just *biz-ness*. Right?"

"Of course, it is." The words came out a little forced, as if she needed to convince herself. "But I still want to look nice."

"You do. So, stop worrying."

Sylvia faced the full-length mirror, stripped out of her shorts, and slipped into a pair of jeans. "Randi, I know that look"—Sylvia spoke to Randi's reflection in the mirror—"that's the look you give when you have something on your mind, but you're not saying."

"*Ay*, Sylvia, leave it. It's nothing."

"It's not nothing. Come on, spill."

Randi rested her coffee cup on the arm of the overstuffed chair. "Truth?"

"Yeah. Truth."

"You might have convinced yourself you're giving Mr. Richy Rich the dime tour of the neighborhood"—Randi wagged an index finger at Sylvia—"but I see what's going on."

Sylvia raised her eyebrows. "What are you talking about?"

"Oh, puh-leez with the innocence. You like him."

"You're hilarious." Sylvia waved her off and stepped back into the closet, pretending to search for an article of clothing. Randi had hit a nerve. She had been thinking about Dale over the past week, and her thoughts weren't all business. She smiled to herself, remembering the hug in the mayor's office and his unique woodsy scent. Somehow, he'd moved from enemy, to frenemy, to something else, but she wasn't sure what.

"Hey, girl. Come out of there. I'm not finished."

Placing a scarf against her neck, Sylvia stepped back into the living room and checked her outfit in the mirror. “Yes?”

Randi shook her head. “Lose the scarf. Now listen to me. I wasn’t trying to be funny. You do know there are tours he can take to visit the historic sections of Washington Heights?”

“And your point is?” Sylvia put a hand on her hip.

“Don’t play dumb. You know what I’m saying. You don’t need to be his personal guide.”

Sylvia stopped talking to Randi’s reflection and turned to face her. “You are my best friend. Correct?”

Randi nodded.

“Then you know me and guys with money don’t mix.” She tossed the scarf onto the couch.

“Yes. Exactly.” Randi swung her feet off the makeshift coffee table and sat forward. “That’s why you gotta keep a respectable distance.”

“I know what I’m doing. I have no intention of making this personal.” Sylvia lifted her face to the ceiling and let out a heavy breath. She was used to Randi’s opinions, and she wasn’t shy about voicing them. More often than not, it’s what she loved about Randi because they mostly agreed on everything. But today, when she was already jittery about seeing Dale, she wished her best friend would keep her thoughts to herself. “It’s not about Dale. It’s simply time for us to stop fighting with the Foresters.” Sylvia held her arms out to the side. “Come on. You, of all people, should be ecstatic. We’re finally getting what we’ve fought so hard for—a brand-new community center. Forester Industries has done a one-hundred-eighty. We should be celebrating.”

Randi placed an elbow on her knee and rested her forehead in the palm of her hand. “I know, you’re right"—she looked up at Sylvia—"it's just…you're like a sister to me…and where Dale Forester is concerned, well, I don't want you to get hurt."

"I love you, too. And I won't." Sylvia pulled Randi out of the chair and embraced her in a long hug.

"Okay. Okay. That's enough." Randi extricated herself from Sylvia's arms. "But if this guy does anything to hurt or upset you, he'll have to deal with me."

Sylvia laughed. "I'm sure the threat of you coming after him will keep him up nights."

Randi looked at her watch. "Okay, go. But I sure hope you know what you're doing."

Sylvia tugged on the hem of her shirt, closed her eyes, and blew out a breath. "That makes two of us."

****

At exactly noon, Sylvia arrived outside Dale's office building on West Fifty-Fifth Street to find him already waiting.

"You're right on time. That's a first." He smiled.

Sylvia put a hand to her chest and gave him a look of mock hurt. But she knew it would be fruitless to protest; punctuality wasn't one of her best attributes. So, she dropped the pretense and shrugged. "Good afternoon."

"Here's the car." Dale's SUV pulled up, and he signaled his driver to stay behind the wheel as he walked to the passenger door.

Sylvia grabbed his arm and tried not to notice the hard biceps beneath his T-shirt or how sexy he looked in his well-worn jeans. "Oh, no, that's not how we're going to roll today." She pulled him back onto the curb. "I'm giving you the full neighborhood experience.

Today, we're going by subway."

Dale's eyes widened a fraction larger than normal, and his jaw went momentarily slack. But he quickly closed his mouth and walked with Sylvia toward the Columbus Circle subway station to catch the uptown A Train. She mentally gave him bonus points for pulling it together. "Here." Sylvia handed Dale a Metro Card.

"What's this?"

"It's how you get into the subway. I bought you a couple of rides when I got to my station this morning."

Dale turned the card over in his hand. "Uh…?"

"Don't worry. Follow me, and I'll show you how to use it."

"Thanks, I think." He gave her a weak smile and followed down the steps toward the turnstile.

Once there, Sylvia swiped her card through the slot and gestured for Dale to do the same.

After two failed attempts, he finally pushed through the turnstile and joined her.

As they threaded their way to the middle of the crowded platform, they came upon a violin trio.

Three young women with their heads and bows moving in unison. They appeared completely lost in their music. In front of them a lone violin case sat open, filled with dollar bills and coins.

Dale reached into his pocket and put a twenty-dollar bill with the rest.

"That was nice of you," Sylvia said.

Dale turned to look at her. "I like to support the arts."

"They're good. Very good. And who doesn't love Stravinsky," Sylvia said.

"So, you're a lover of the arts, too?" Dale raised an

eyebrow and smiled with one corner of his mouth.

"Don't look so surprised." Sylvia gave him a playful shove. "I had a well-rounded education. Besides, my father was a classical music nut. I learned everything I know from him. He also insisted I learn to play the piano."

"Do you still play?"

Sylvia shook her head. "I'd love to, but I don't have a piano anymore."

"Why not?"

Raising her voice to be heard over the rumble of the downtown train pulling in across the platform, Sylvia leaned close. "It belonged to my parents. They lived in a large apartment, unlike my one-room studio. And sadly, I didn't have the space." She shrugged. "The choice was between my foldout couch or a baby grand. Since I couldn't sleep on the piano, the couch won."

Dale leaned in. "Do you miss it?"

"Every day." Sylvia's voice was thick with emotion. The piano wasn't the only thing she was missing. Dale gave her hand a gentle squeeze, and his look of empathy had her taking a step back. She shook her head. "It's all good."

A swoosh of hot air rushed in, and Sylvia pulled Dale back from the platform's edge as the uptown express train screeched into the station. Holding on to his arm, she yelled over the noise. "You're not yet fluent in *subway*, but you'll catch on."

When the train stopped, she pulled him farther to the side to avoid being trampled by the dozens of straphangers spilling out of its doors. Stepping aboard and moving through the still-crowded car, they inched their way toward a small patch of space in the middle and grabbed onto the overhead bar as the doors closed.

Several seconds after pulling out of the station, the train took a sharp curve, throwing Sylvia off balance and into Dale. Unexpected electricity shot through her as she felt his arm slip around her waist to prevent her from falling. Quickly righting herself, she gave him an embarrassed smile and lowered her eyes.

For Sylvia, as with most New Yorkers, riding the subway was a matter of convenience and expediency. The Manhattan Transit Authority trains got you where you needed to go faster than any other mode of transportation. However, it required a trade-off; convenience and speed over metal wheels scraping against metal tracks, making it nearly impossible to have a conversation without yelling. Usually, the deafening noise bothered her. Today, however, she was relieved the screeching was too loud to speak. It gave her time to get a grip on those jittery, dancing butterflies in her lower regions. These were new sensations, and she could only attribute them to being physically close to Dale. Maybe Randi was right. Maybe she did like him more than she should. Why *had* she decided to be his personal tour guide?

For the duration of the ride, Sylvia held onto the overhead pole, smiled, and worked hard at looking anywhere but at Dale.

When the train pulled into the Broadway and 168th Street station, she let out a relieved breath.

"Okay. This is us." Sylvia extended her hand toward the opening doors in an after-you fashion, letting Dale exit first.

Stepping onto the platform, she shook her head several times, as if saying no to someone who wasn't there. Did she really spend the entire subway ride avoiding Dale's gaze? *Ug-h-h-h-h.* She gave another quick shake of her head. The purpose of the afternoon was to show Dale the neighborhood…nothing more.

Dale was waiting in the center of the platform.

Sylvia gave him a polite smile and pointed in the direction of a long, steep stairway leading up to the street.

In front of them, a young, thin woman with a baby in a stroller, and a toddler on one hip, was having difficulty navigating the stairs.

"Can I help you?" Dale asked.

But the woman gave a wary look and held her child tighter.

"It's okay. We just want to help." Sylvia smiled.

Looking from Dale to Sylvia, the woman returned the smile. "Okay. Thank you." She put her toddler down and lifted her infant.

Sylvia held the little girl's hand and followed the mother up the stairs.

Dale lifted the stroller and made the long climb to the street level.

Once the infant was back safely in the stroller, the mother thanked them and waved goodbye.

"How would she have managed if we hadn't helped?" Dale asked.

"Someone else would have. New Yorkers are friendly that way." Sylvia took Dale's elbow and steered him in the direction of Broadway. "Come on. We've got places to go." As they walked the avenue, Sylvia surreptitiously watched Dale from the corner of her eye. Having grown up in the neighborhood, she was accustomed to the sights and sounds, and she hardly noticed most things anymore.

But Dale looked around wide-eyed.

The fruit stands and vegetable carts took up one side of the sidewalk, while the other side was crammed with dozens of mom-and-pop stores selling everything from food to clothing and from furniture to fortune-telling.

“This place rivals the crowds in downtown Manhattan during rush hour,” Dale said.

Sylvia nodded. “Yeah. It’s Saturday. Most people are off work, and this is the only time they can run their errands. You know, food shop, laundry, and buy whatever they need for the week.”

“It’s lively,” Dale said. “I see what you mean by neighborhood.”

“Yes, but walking a couple of blocks is by no means the extent of the tour.”

“So where are you taking me?”

“You’ll find out.” Sylvia winked. Her words came out in a singsong lilt. Before Dale could open his mouth to speak, Sylvia put a finger to his lips. “No questions, just follow. You think you can do that?” She instantly regretted touching him. *Dang, what is with these stooooopid butterflies?* “Let’s go.” She turned away to hide the heat creeping up her face.

Chapter 12

Dale tried to keep up with Sylvia as she zigzagged her way through the pedestrian traffic. But each storefront beckoned for his attention, and he nearly face-planted on the pavement when he skirted a clothing rack being wheeled onto the sidewalk. Quickly righting himself, he jogged to catch up with her.

They walked north on Fort Washington Avenue for several blocks until Sylvia stopped at a colorful storefront. "Do you know how to ride?" She tilted her chin toward the bicycles in the window.

"Of course, I do." Dale laughed, thinking this was the last thing in the world they'd be doing today.

"Good. We're going in. Follow me."

Dale had never been in a store this small or crowded with merchandise. Dozens of bicycles stood upright on either side of the single aisle. Dozens more in all styles and colors hung from the ceiling. Eye-level steel shelving held helmets, water bottles, racks, headlamps, safety vests, and various other bicycle accessories. He followed Sylvia down the aisle, keeping his hands close to his sides for fear of knocking merchandise over. "These all look like they're for sale."

"Yup. They are. The rentals are back here." Sylvia stopped at the counter and rang the bell next to the register.

"Be right there." The voice came from behind a

wall of bikes stacked on metal bars three rows high. Within seconds, a short, stout man with dark hair emerged, wiping grease from his hands.

"Hey, Gabriel."

The man smiled, and his eyes lit up. "Sylvia! I haven't seen you in a while. How are you?"

"Great. How are you? How's the family?"

"No complaints, everyone's fine. Oh, did you hear? Mickey got accepted to Fordham University."

"I heard. That's fantastic news. *Felicidades*!" Sylvia said.

"Thanks. Yeah, we're so proud of him." Gabriel beamed. "So, what can I do for you today?"

"This is my friend, Dale. I'm showing him around the neighborhood, and I thought we'd do the tour on bikes."

"Nice to meet you, Dale. I'd shake your hand"—he wiggled his greased, stained fingers —"but as you can see, I was just fixing one of the rentals in the back." Gabriel looked Dale up and down. "You're about six feet?"

"Six-two." Dale straightened and tucked his hands into his pockets.

"I have the perfect bike for you. And Sylvia"—Gabriel called over his shoulder as he headed toward the back of the shop—"I already know which one you like."

"Do you come here often?" Dale asked.

"Not as much as I used to, but I know Gabriel and his family. His kids used the community center. And my apartment is too small to keep a bike, so it's easier to rent one when I want to spend a lazy weekend riding along the river." Sylvia leaned against the counter.

“Why not rent one of the bikes the city provides along most avenues?”

“Because they’re too far downtown. Besides, ever heard of supporting local businesses?”

“Here we go.” Gabriel rolled out a sleek, dark blue racer and passed it to Dale. “I’ll be right back with yours, Sylvia.”

Holding the bike in one hand, Dale gave it the once-over. A few years ago, he belonged to a bike club. They’d meet on Saturdays in Central Park, and they would ride the trails. That was before his father died. In the last year, Dale had gotten the idea life wasn’t supposed to be fun. But that all seemed to be changing. He smiled to himself. This was turning out to be a better day than he expected.

Moments later, Gabriel produced a model in bubblegum pink.

“Oh, wow,” Dale said. “I didn’t see that coming. It’s like from what, the 1960s?”

“Very observant,” Sylvia acknowledged. “I rent this one every time. Isn’t it the coolest?”

“I was thinking more along the lines of slow. Well, at least compared to this one.” Dale tapped the handlebars of his ride.

“Oh, come on. It’s not slow. It’s retro.” The pink bike sported fringes hanging from the ends of its handlebars and a white wicker basket above the front fender. “And we’re not racing, so this will be just fine.”

“Does it work?” Dale asked.

Sylvia laughed. “It’s got two wheels and a couple of pedals. Of course, it works. Besides, Gabriel keeps his bikes in excellent condition.” Sylvia winked at the store owner and put her credit card on the counter.

"No, please. I've got this." Dale reached into the back pocket of his jeans.

"Nope. Not gonna happen." Sylvia nudged him out of the way. "This was my idea, so it's my treat."

Dale had never allowed a woman to pay for anything. It surprised and secretly delighted him.

They rolled their rides out the front door and strapped on the obligatory safety helmets. Sylvia pushed off first, leading the way down the block. They rode north, single file for a couple of miles, past apartment buildings, stores, and churches until they came to a narrow, elevated bridge known as the Dykman Street Viaduct. They joined other New Yorkers already enjoying the sunshine—dozens of people walking, several on bikes, a few rollerblading, and a couple of kids on skateboards.

As he rode farther across the bridge, the pedestrian traffic thinned, making it possible for them to ride side by side. "So, where are you taking me?"

"To The Cloisters. Ever been?"

"Actually, that's one museum I've not been to. I'm more of an Impressionist kinda guy. The Middle Ages never really did it for me." Dale continued to pedal only to find Sylvia was no longer next to him. Squeezing the hand brakes, he stopped and looked back. "Is everything all right?"

Several feet behind him, Sylvia stood, straddling her bike with her hands on her hips. "If you've never been, how can you say you don't like it? Ever study the Middle Ages?"

Dale shook his head.

"Seriously?" She raised her eyebrows so high they disappeared under her helmet. "Then you're in for an experience. Look"—she pointed to a medieval structure peeking out from behind the trees about fifty yards ahead—"that's The Cloisters." Sylvia walked her bike, stopping inches from his side. "How can you not want to explore a reconstructed fourteenth century monastery?" She poked him in the chest. "You, my friend, are clueless as to what you've been missing, and I'm about to show you." She laughed and pedaled off.

Dale shook his head and rubbed his chest where she'd prodded him.

"Hey, what are you doing?" Sylvia motioned for him to catch up. "Come on."

Dale pushed off and pedaled after her. He'd been looking forward to spending an afternoon with Sylvia, not with some centuries-old relics. What had he gotten himself into?

****

The moment they stepped inside the museum, Sylvia felt wrapped in warmth. This was one of her favorite places in all of New York City, because it reminded her of the Saturday afternoons she'd spent here with her father.

The museum offered an audio tour Sylvia insisted they purchase. While she knew practically every corner of The Cloisters by heart, she wanted Dale to have the full Middle Ages experience, and the tour provided a deeper understanding of the various artifacts, paintings, tapestries, and altars. "Something about this period in history seems to relax me," Sylvia said.

"You mean having no running water, toilet paper, or cell phones?" Dale smirked. "You find that thought relaxing, do you?"

"Ha. Ha." Sylvia grinned and put on the walking

tour headphones, motioning for Dale to do the same. They walked toward a jeweled chalice perched on a pedestal. Over the next hour, Sylvia noticed Dale's increased interest as they progressed through the tour.

Dale stopped several times to engage her in conversation about specific pieces and to comment on the world-famous unicorn tapestries.

"I told you this period in history shouldn't be overlooked. It wasn't all black plagues and hundred-year wars."

Dale laughed.

She removed her headphones. "Come on, let's go outside." Hooking her arm into his, she steered him toward the famous Cloister gardens overlooking the Hudson River. She smiled as they stepped out into the sunlight. "What do you think?"

"Fascinating for sure, but honestly, I'm still not a huge fan of medieval art." He nodded toward the river. "However, this view is remarkable."

Sylvia looked up and nudged him with her shoulder. "Okay, so you're not a convert yet, but look at these gardens." She pointed out the lavender plants, white roses, red carnations, mint, and coriander. The fragrance was a mixture of sweet and pungent.

"It's impressive," Dale said.

Sylvia put her hands on her hips and stared. "Impressive? Is that all you have to say?"

"Okay, they're beautiful. Is that what you want to hear?" Dale dipped his chin and pointed to his chest. "Look at me. Do I look like the type to visit gardens and gush?"

"But you're missing the point of this particular garden." Sylvia held her arms out to the side and turned in place. “Look. Take a good look. These aren’t planted purely for beauty. These flowers and herbs were used to cure illnesses. I mean, it’s not like in the 1300s you could run down to the local chain drugstore and buy a bottle of aspirin or fill a prescription for antibiotics. So, they used what Mother Nature provided.”

Dale chuckled. “Okay, you got me there.”

“Look over there.” Sylvia pointed toward a garden bed a few feet away. “That’s lavender, used for headaches and nerves, and still used in aromatherapy today. Personally, I can’t get enough of the scent.” She took in a deep breath. “Ahhhhh, lovely.” Sylvia walked to the next bed.

Dale stepped up beside her and took in a deep breath, as Sylvia had done a moment ago. “Smells familiar.”

“That’s mint. Helpful with digestive issues”—she pointed to the next bed—“and here you have coriander—used to reduce fevers.”

“How do you know so much about herbs and plants?”

“My father introduced me to this museum when I was six years old. This was our favorite father-daughter place. We did the garden tour a couple of times, and I wanted to know more, so he took me to the library, and I looked up a lot of stuff.” She paused, swallowing hard. “I miss him.” She looked away and headed toward the stone wall railing overlooking the river.

Dale was soon standing by her side.

She turned to face him, squinting against the sun. “I’m okay. I needed a minute.”

“I get it. It’s hard when you lose someone you love.” Dale rested a hand on her shoulder. “The loss never seems to go away."

Sylvia felt a warmth rush through her and closed her eyes.

"You're right about one thing," Dale said.

"What's that?"

"The view is amazing."

Sylvia gave a knowing smile, stepped away from his touch, and looked out over the Hudson to The Palisades on the New Jersey side. The vista was breathtaking. "Yeah, you can see pretty far."

"Standing here, you almost feel like you're not in New York City anymore," Dale said.

"Exactly." Sylvia took in the view. "This is my special place when I want to sort out problems or make decisions."

"I can see how it could help clear your head."

"This view somehow makes the possibilities seem endless. When I was a little girl, I wished I had a boat and could sail up the Hudson." Sylvia closed her eyes, remembering the feeling of excitement she had each time she and her father stood on this very spot.

They were silent for a while, and Sylvia sensed Dale's gaze was on her and not the view. "What?" She turned toward him. "Why are you staring?" She swiped at her nose. "Do I have something on my face?"

"No." Dale laughed. "I'm staring because you're as beautiful as the view."

His words surprised her, and that warm feeling returned, along with a pesky stomach flip.

Unexpectedly, Dale took hold of her hand and slowly leaned in until their lips were inches apart.

Her heart fluttered at his touch, and her eyelids closed as she lifted her face toward his. Sylvia's heart was performing somersaults until Randi's voice popped into her head. *Seriously? Honey, just stop. You can't fall for this guy*. Sylvia's eyelids flew open. "It's time to go."

Dale blinked. "What? Where?"

Sylvia stepped back. "You'll see." She forced herself to keep a light tone, hoping her emotions wouldn't betray her. Falling for Dale was not an option. She had no use for rich, powerful men who were accustomed to getting what they wanted. They were complete opposites. Becoming involved would only end in heartache. Somehow, she had to put distance between them. The last thing she needed was another Julian disaster.

Chapter 13

The afternoon had been relaxed and exhilarating all at once, and Dale wanted to get back the easiness he and Sylvia had experienced for most of the day. In fact, everything had been perfect until he'd tried to kiss her. Seeing her pull away, he knew he'd made a mistake. He hoped it wasn't irreparable.

They headed out of the museum and toward their chained bikes.

Dale spent longer than necessary, busying himself with unlocking the chain while he thought of something to say. "Uh, you know, when you suggested I get to know the neighborhood, I certainly didn't think you had The Cloisters in mind."

"I know. Crazy, right? Not your typical get-to-know-the-neighborhood tour. But it's one of the treasures in this area, and it shouldn't be missed. Even if I haven't turned you into a medieval art convert."

He wanted to say she could convert him into anything, but she'd likely take offense. So, he strapped on his helmet and kept it simple. "I wouldn't exactly say I've been transformed, but I did learn a few things. And, despite my reservations, I very much enjoyed myself."

"Good. I'm glad," Sylvia said. "Let's head back. I know a shortcut."

They pedaled the few miles back to Gabriel's

bicycle shop. Smiling as they rode down upper Broadway, he thought how natural being with Sylvia felt. There were no pretenses. No posing.

Over the years, Dale had dated at least a dozen women, and, if he were being honest, he was aware they'd primarily been interested in his wealth and privilege. Sylvia seemed to be different. He noticed she'd been happy to take her time during the day and not rush as if she were marking off the next item on her to-do list. She hadn't once checked her reflection in a storefront window or on her phone, in case the paparazzi decided to take a *gotcha* photo. He was certain the last thing on her mind was being tagged on social media with the heir to the Forester empire. The fact that she was wearing a helmet, without a care for what effect it might have on her hair, spoke volumes. It wasn't something the women he knew would do. In a word, Sylvia was refreshing.

A car horn honked. "Hey, watch where you're going!" a red-faced man yelled as he drove past.

Dale swerved back into the bike lane, his heart skipping a couple of beats. Riding a bike in New York City was not for the faint of heart. He needed to get his mind out of the clouds and back on the road. *Pedal, pedal, right, left, right, left. Keep your eyes on the road. Pedal, pedal, right, left, right, left.*

He tried to stay focused by repeating the mantra over and over, but he couldn't help his thoughts from drifting. *Pedal, pedal, her chestnut-colored hair. Come on, stay focused. Pedal, pedal. Her plum-colored lips. Her lips!* Dale recalled his attempt to kiss her on the terrace of The Cloisters and silently groaned. *What was I thinking*?

After their dinner at Le Jardin, she hadn't phoned him or so much as sent him a text for nearly a week. A short while ago, she'd pulled away from the almost-kiss. All evidence pointed to the fact she had no interest in him. They would be working together, and she was simply showing him the neighborhood. Nothing more. Realizing the truth, Dale sighed and kept pedaling.

Twenty minutes later, they finally arrived at the bike shop and returned the rentals. As they stepped outside the shop, he was the first to speak. "That was a lot of fun. Can't say I've ever done anything like that before." He checked his watch. "So, I guess I should call my driver."

"Wait. You're not leaving just yet?" Sylvia held onto his forearm. "I promised you the full neighborhood experience, and that's what I'm going to deliver."

"I…I…don't want to monopolize…your time." It surprised Dale she wanted to spend more time with him.

Sylvia raised her eyebrows. "Do you have somewhere more important to be?"

There were a hundred things he needed to do at the office—projects to review, proposals to approve, cost reports to authorize, but none of it mattered. He'd rather spend time with her than with paperwork and phone calls. "All right then. What's next on the agenda?"

"Are you hungry?"

"Starving." Dale unconsciously placed a hand on his stomach.

"Good, because you're in for a treat. I'm taking you to the best Puerto Rican restaurant in the city, and it's only a block from here." Sylvia turned and headed down 168th Street toward Broadway.

"Would this be one of those culinary hideaways you mentioned at dinner the other night?" Dale took extra steps to keep up with her.

"You joke, but wait until you taste the food. You'll be asking yourself why you haven't eaten there before." She pointed across the street to *La Cocina* in the middle of the block ahead of them.

The traffic light turned green. Dale felt a pull as Sylvia grabbed his hand, and they ran across the wide expanse of Broadway.

The moment they set foot in the restaurant, the aromas enveloped him. The delicious fragrance of garlic cooking in oil made his stomach rumble.

"*Buenos días, mi hija. como va todo?*" A petite woman in her early fifties greeted them and pulled Sylvia into a warm embrace. "*¿Quién es*?" She lifted her chin in the stranger's direction.

"This is my friend, Dale." Sylvia put a hand in the crook of his arm. "Dale, this is Carmen, and that's her husband, Luís."

A short, bearded man rushed up, hugged Sylvia, and shook Dale's hand. "*Encantado*. Any friend of Sylvia's is a friend of ours."

"Your usual spot, *mi hija?*" Carmen asked.

"Yes, please."

They were ushered to a table for two by the front windows. They settled into their chairs, and Luís handed them menus. "Something to drink?"

Sylvia turned to Dale. "Would it offend you if I did all the ordering?"

"Order away. I'm in your hands." Dale relaxed his shoulders. The easy feeling between them was back, and the knot in his stomach eased.

"Do you like beer?" Sylvia asked

Dale smiled. "Sure."

"Great, we'll have *dos cervezas*," Sylvia said.

Luís pulled out a pen and order pad from his apron pocket.

"And to start, we'll have one order of *alcapurrias*, and *bacalaitos*. Next, *ensalada con aquacate*, and then…oh, yes, the *pernil con arroz con gandules* and *mofongo*."

"That's it?" Luís' face was expressionless. "You sure you're not expecting more people?"

"Ha, ha. Very funny. First, you know I love to eat." Sylvia began ticking items off on her fingers. "Secondly, this is Dale's first experience with authentic Puerto Rican food, and I want him to taste all my favorites. And thirdly, whatever we don't finish"—she gave a toothy smile—"I get the doggy bag."

"I tell you what"—Luís tucked the pad and pen into his apron—"why don't I bring you small plates of everything, like a tasting menu? This way, Dale can try it all without having to take a bicarbonate of soda afterward."

"*¡Perfecto!* You're the best." Sylvia squeezed Luís' hand.

He turned and headed for the kitchen.

"Can I ask what we'll be eating?"

Sylvia wiggled her eyebrows. "You are about to experience mouthfuls of deliciousness."

Dale grinned. He was starving, having skipped breakfast and lunch, so at this point, even fried cardboard might taste good.

"Trust me. You're going to love it. And whatever

you don't like, you don't have to eat." Sylvia gave a one-arm shrug.

Dale leaned forward. "I trust you because it looks like you're on pretty good terms with the owners. I guess you come here often?"

Sylvia's gaze swept the room. "For as long as I can remember, this place has been a part of my life. It reminds me of my parents. We ate many meals here."

"If the food tastes half as good as it smells, I don't wonder why."

"You know, places like this—family-run businesses—they're one of the reasons I love The Heights. It's a community." Sylvia sighed and looked out of the window.

"What's the matter?" Dale cocked his head.

"It makes me sad."

"What does?"

"Places like these are being bought out, and the intimacy of the neighborhood is changing. You know, like the personality is being stripped away. It's like we're becoming…homogenized." Sylvia waved a hand. "Ahhh, never mind. Forget it. Today isn't a day for soap boxes."

"Are you perfectly well, Ms. Ramirez? I mean, it's not like you to hold back on a thought." Dale slid his chair closer. "Come on, let loose. Tell me what you were going to say. Besides, I'm hungry, you're hungry, and we've got nothing else to do but wait for our food. I'm kinda like a sure thing. You know, a captive audience."

Sylvia put her elbows on the table and pursed her lips. "Okay, Mr. Captive Audience of One, here's what I think. I think it's a crying shame we go from family-run businesses to upscale corporate coffeehouses where the cost of a cup of espresso is more than a whole pound of coffee beans at the *bodega* up the block." She blew a stray hair from her face.

Dale sensed she was just getting started, and a rush of admiration filled him. He'd never met a person more passionate about their beliefs. He smiled, knowing it was her zest for life that captivated his thoughts.

"Are you smirking at me? Already?"

Straightening in his chair, Dale shook his head. "Go on. I'm listening. Promise." He held up three fingers like a Boy Scout.

Sylvia huffed. "Look, getting rid of the corner delis and replacing them with organic specialty stores selling overpriced lettuce sandwiches is ridiculous. Look around. This is a working-class neighborhood." Her voice rose. "Don't get me wrong. Organic is a good thing, but it's expensive. That's why I believe creating a garden as part of the community center would be an essential addition."

"Listen, I don't want to dampen your dreams"—Dale held up a hand—"but first, we need to make sure there's enough room for the housing *and* the new center now that we've changed the plans."

Sylvia paused. "My intention is not to make you feel bad, because I know how much you've done to make the center happen. So please, try not to take offense at what I'm about to say."

Dale nodded.

"You don't know what it feels like not to be able to afford basic necessities, like food."

Dale shifted in his seat. This was not the first time he had heard that remark. But it was the first time it had made him uncomfortable.

"Look out there." Sylvia pointed to the street. "You see all the cars, the traffic, and the people? There's no green space in this part of town. No place to grow anything. So, people in this part of town buy their produce from the grocery store." Sylvia took in a deep breath and leaned closer. "There's no doubt organic produce is better than anything grown with pesticides. But most people in this area can't afford it. And believe me, there's a big difference between a freshly picked tomato right off the vine and something artificially grown in a hothouse and shipped half-ripe."

Dale couldn't take his gaze off her. Yes, she was saying things that made him more uncomfortable than he liked, but the fire in her eyes was an irresistible flame. For the moment, he didn't care if he got burned.

"I'm not telling you anything you don't already know," Sylvia said. "But if the new community center had a garden with plots for people in the neighborhood, they'd have several months of fresh, organic fruits and vegetables. I mean, we could maybe even plant several apple trees—"

"Whoa." Dale raised a hand. "You had me at garden. You lost me at orchard." But her passion was contagious, and Dale found himself wanting what she wanted. "A community garden sounds terrific. Let's see if we can get the planning committee to agree."

Before she could argue, and Dale was beginning to understand Sylvia Ramirez could argue about anything, Luís arrived with the appetizers.

He placed two beers on the table with a platter of starters. "These are *alcapurrias.*" Luis pointed to a grouping of golden fritters. "They're green plantains, stuffed with meat, and then fried. And these"—he pointed to the other half of the platter—"are the *bacalaitos.* All I'll say is they are a codfish delight." Luís winked and gave a chef's kiss. "*Buen provecho.*" Giving a slight bow he turned and walked toward the kitchen.

"What does that mean?" Dale whispered.

"It's the same as saying *bon appétit*, only in Spanish. Anyway, no more talk about the new center or organic gardens. I'm stepping off my soapbox for the rest of the day. Let's just enjoy this meal." She pointed toward the plate on his left. "Start with the *bacalaitos.* They're best eaten hot."

"Say no more. The aroma alone is making my salivary glands work overtime." Dale put several on his plate, took a bite, and moaned. "Oh, man, the salty, crispy, spicy flavor. This is so good."

"That's quite a description. You sound like you're hosting a television cooking show." Sylvia laughed. "But I'm glad you like it."

As the meal progressed, they moved from topic to topic. For almost two hours, they laughed and talked as if they were on a first date. Dale worked hard to keep it casual but ached to reach over and take hold of Sylvia's hand. He didn't want this time together to end. But they'd already had coffee and dessert, and people were waiting for tables.

Sylvia stretched her arms behind her head. "Well, now that you've been properly fed, it's time for an after-dinner walk."

"I'm not sure I can move. I think I'm in a food coma."

"Me, too." Sylvia laughed.

"You were right, this place is a gem, and it won't be the last time I eat here. I'll get the check."

"But—"

"No"—Dale shook his head—"you got the bike rentals. I got this." He raised a hand in the air to get Luís's attention.

Luís nodded and sent over a server.

Once Dale paid the bill, they made their way through the maze of tables toward the front entrance. The atmosphere in the now-crowded restaurant was like a family gathering. But it wasn't like any family gathering he'd ever known.

"There's Luís and Carmen." Sylvia tugged on his shirt sleeve. "Come. I want to say goodbye."

Luís and Carmen were standing by the register and greeted them with warm smiles.

"That was delicious. I'm completely stuffed." Dale patted his stomach. "Thank you."

"We're glad you enjoyed it." Luís smiled. "You're welcome back anytime."

"Thank you." Sylvia put her arms around Luís and Carmen in a group hug. "This was great." She stepped back and tilted her head in Dale's direction. "I think we have a convert."

"You most certainly do. The *pernil* was the best-tasting pork I've ever eaten. Thanks again." Dale smiled and reached for the door.

But Sylvia didn't move. "Is Miguel moving around yet?"

The conversation lasted a couple of minutes, and Dale was relieved to hear Miguel was making progress and would be back apprenticing in the kitchen next week.

Once again, Sylvia hugged them both. "*Adiós.*"

Dale reached for the door.

"Oh, Sylvia," Carmen called. "The church's clothing drive is next week. Can I count on you to help tag the donations?"

"Yes, of course. I'll call you, and we'll work out the details." Sylvia kissed Carmen on the cheek.

Dale smiled, nodded goodbye, and reached for the door again.

"*Ay*, Sylvia, I forgot"—Luís snapped his fingers—"we haven't talked about the block party yet. Did you have the playlist worked out?"

"Luís, don't worry. It's all set. But maybe I should email you the link, and you can let me know if you want to add anything."

Luís grinned. "Hey, great idea. And you know what—"

Dale cleared his throat, wondering if goodbye meant the same in all languages. He came from a world of air kisses and quick farewells. This was not that.

Sylvia turned and smiled. "Oh, sorry, Dale. This is your standard Puerto Rican goodbye. It typically takes at least ten minutes."

Dale chuckled. "Thanks for the heads-up. I'll remember for next time." But he knew all he'd remember was her smile and how it lit up his universe. It surprised the heck out of him. A few weeks ago, he'd wanted nothing more than to be rid of this woman. Now, he realized he couldn't get enough of her. And why did that feel like trouble?

Chapter 14

For the next two weeks, community volunteers worked alongside Sylvia and Randi, cleaning out the community center basement, packing equipment, sorting files, taking inventory of salvageable furniture, and readying the building for the wrecking ball.

On the last day, Sylvia thanked the friends and neighbors who'd come to help. When she returned to her office, she found Randi sitting on the floor, sealing the few remaining boxes.

"You know," Randi said, "under normal circumstances, I might be sad to say goodbye"—she looked up but didn't stop taping—"but my honest reaction is joy."

Sylvia raised an eyebrow.

"Come on, gurl. You gotta admit, this place put the *d* in dilapidated, the *o* in outdated, and the *g* in good riddance."

"All right, already." Sylvia groaned. "Stop yourself. I get it."

"Hmph." Randi made a tsking sound. "You know I'm right."

"I'm not disagreeing, but I'm still going to miss coming here every day. Man, five years went by fast." Sylvia looked around the room. She'd spent many long nights dreaming and planning in this office.

Randi waved a hand in dismissal. "Stop being so

nostalgic."

"I can't help it"—Sylvia lifted her arms out to the sides to encompass the room—"pieces of our souls are in this place."

Randi shrugged. "Okay, you got me there. But pieces of our souls aren't the only things we're leaving behind."

"Huh?"

"Girl, we've cleaned up cuts, disinfected scraped knees, exterminated mice, and repaired broken computers. And in the process, left bits and pieces of ourselves, and we've—" She stopped herself mid-sentence and shook her head. "It doesn't matter anymore. Time to move on." She stood and waved Sylvia over. "Come here, you. Let's get one last selfie." Taking her phone from her back pocket, Randi leaned against the desk, put her head against Sylvia's, and stretched out her right arm. "Okay, *sonrisa*!" She pressed the button on her phone. "Well, that's the last picture of us in this place."

"Thanks for the memories." A sense of sadness enveloped Sylvia, and she plucked a tissue from the box on her desk and blew her nose. "I'm going to finish putting away these files."

"Hold up. Let me make sure the pic's good before you start packing again." Randi paused. "Yup, that works. I'm gonna post it, hashtag out-of-work."

"Ha, ha. Not funny. Plus, it's not even true." Sylvia stretched a strip of packing tape across a box of files. "We'll only be unemployed for one week." She'd been thrilled when Forester Industries offered them a consulting gig on the Washington Heights Project. It meant she'd truly be involved in the planning and design. "You know, you could be a little grateful we don't have to collect unemployment."

Randi snorted.

Sylvia shot her a look.

"What?" Randi asked.

"He did not need to offer us jobs."

"Yeah. He did." Randi nodded her head several times. "He knew the only way to get things done in this neighborhood was to have us working on the project. It's a smart move."

Sylvia took a deep breath. "So why the snort? Why do you hate him so much?"

"I don't hate him. Look, let's drop it, okay?"

Sylvia still couldn't understand Randi's continued blatant disapproval of Dale Forester. With all he was doing for the community, she thought Randi would have warmed to him by now. After all, it had been her idea they work with Dale. She wanted to sort this out, but now was not the time. "Okay"—she brushed her hands against the front of her jeans—"hurry up, the moving vans will be here at two."

"*¡Ay, paciencia*! Give me a sec to add more tags to this pic."

Sylvia put a hand on her hip and watched as Randi's thumbs flew across her phone's keyboard.

Randi looked up and pursed her lips. "What? Why the stare? You know, the more followers, the more fundraising possibilities."

Sylvia shook her head and chuckled. As usual, Randi was right.

At two o'clock on the dot, the movers arrived and began carting out furniture, file boxes, computers, desks, chairs, kitchen paraphernalia, and sports equipment. It would all be used at the new center.

Randi had wanted to leave everything behind and purchase brand-new furniture and equipment to go along with a brand-new building. But Sylvia had convinced her plenty of other purchases required their money-raising skills. Why waste time on items in good condition?

Three hours later, they stood on the front steps. Sylvia's eyes filled with tears as she watched the last cartons loaded into the remaining moving van for storage.

Randi put an arm around Sylvia's shoulders. "Get it together, girl. You're the one who said this is only temporary."

Sylvia reached into the pocket of her jeans, pulled out a tissue, and blew her nose. "I know." She sniffed. "So many things have happened in this building. So many good things."

"And we'll create more memories in the new building." Randi patted her on the back. "Now, let's lock up this place and get a drink."

One last time, they walked from room to room, turning off lights, closing windows, and locking doors. The bulldozers were set to tear everything down in a couple of days, but in the meantime, why invite vandalism?

They stepped outside to the high, beeping sound of trucks backing up into the large vacant lot across the street. The big semis worked in a coordinated dance, depositing Forester Industries' cargo trailers throughout the bare space. Once the project got underway, they would serve as the temporary working offices of the engineers, architects, and construction managers.

Off to the side, another, smaller truck came to a stop. Four men got out and began unloading the steel posts needed for the tall, chain-link fence that would circle the perimeter.

"There's our new home." Sylvia pointed toward the trailers. "I can't wait to see what it's like to work in one of those."

"Yeah, six months in a tin can. Can't wait," Randi said.

It would take much longer for the entire development to be completed. But Sylvia and Randi had spent several weeks raising money to create a temporary center located on one floor of the National Guard Armory a few blocks away. While the development was under construction, the temporary center would provide a hot meal to people in the community who needed it, offer health care services, and a computer room. The neighborhood kids would have a chance to use the Armory's basketball court twice a week. It wasn't an ideal situation, but it was something until their permanent space was built.

"Okay, I've seen enough. Let's go get that drink." Sylvia hooked her arm through Randi's and headed west toward Broadway. They were halfway up the block when Sylvia's phone chimed. "Hold on, maybe it's the storage facility." She reached in her back pocket and pulled out her phone. To her surprise, it was a text from Dale.

—Have you moved out yet?—

She smiled and quickly typed back,

—Yes. Sad emoji. Going to drown my sorrows now. Wine glass emogi—

"Who are you texting? That's not the storage

facility, is it?" Randi asked.

Sylvia shook her head. "It's no one."

"It's not no one." Randi stepped back, shaking her head. "I know everyone you know."

"It's not important." Sylvia pursed her lips, trying to hide her smile.

"That look on your face doesn't say unimportant."

"What makes you say that?"

Randi stopped in the middle of the sidewalk and faced Sylvia. "Okay, you got that thing you do with your face every time Dale's name is mentioned. You have been doing it for the last three weeks."

"What thing with my face?" Sylvia raised an eyebrow, trying to cover up the fact her feelings were showing. "Dale's name wasn't even mentioned."

"Oh, my bad." Randi rolled her eyes. "Girl, his name doesn't need to be mentioned. You only need to be thinking about him. I bet money that text is from him. Let me see." Randi made a move to grab Sylvia's phone.

Sylvia put it behind her back. "What's wrong with you, Randi? Stop it!"

Randi stood, unmoving with her hand outstretched, fingers wiggling in a give-it-here motion.

Sylvia sighed. "Okay, fine. It was a text from Dale, but it's perfectly innocent. See." She thrust her phone at Randi. "He's in Buffalo at a site and wants to make sure the move went smoothly."

Randi shook her head. "Man, I knew it. You're crushing on this guy. This guy, who is now our boss. This guy, who, last I checked, is still a Forester. What is wrong with you?" She stamped a foot. "Did you pack your brain with those boxes? I told you to take his help.

Take his money. But that's it. Nothing else should be on the table. Least of all you and him."

"There is no crushing going on. None." Heat rose to her face as she spoke the lie. "Now, can we go get that drink?"

Randi shook her head and put her hands in her pockets. "This is going to be one long, hot summer. That's all I can say." She turned and continued toward Broadway.

Sylvia hurried to catch up. With each step, she worked at suppressing a smile threatening to take up every square inch of her face. Acting as if she didn't care was becoming increasingly impossible. Each time she thought of Dale's penetrating green eyes, and dark hair that seemed to fall in such a relaxed way around his face, her stomach performed triple flips.

Randi had no idea she'd gotten to know Dale on a more personal level. None of it had been planned—only a few meetings at his office to review construction plans and space allocation. But a couple of the sessions had gone longer than expected, and Dale had graciously offered to order dinner, so they could continue working. Sylvia found she couldn't refuse.

One night, while eating pizza and reviewing square footage, she had admired his collection of miniature cars. "Are those antique toys?"

"Actually," he said, "they're model cars made to look antique. My father and I made them. When I was a kid, we used to spend weekends creating miniature villages." Dale's face lit up as he told Sylvia about the many hours he and his father spent together. "The models on the shelf are pieces of one village. I keep them there to remind me of the special times in my life and to remind me to be like my father and follow in his footsteps. He was an exceptional man."

"It would seem we're alike in that way," Sylvia said.

"In what way?"

"We both had wonderful fathers to emulate."

Dale reached over and took her hand, giving it a gentle squeeze.

The feel of his hand over hers, and the compassion in his eyes made her heart melt.

"Hey, girl." Randi tapped Sylvia's arm. "Where'd ya go? I asked if you wanted to go to City Lights or Jubilee?"

Sylvia shrugged. "Whatever."

"Okay, now I know something's up cuz you *always* have an opinion."

Sylvia stopped walking. Randi was too smart. The last thing she needed was Randi all up in her business. If her best friend in the world knew how she felt or that she'd spent one too many nights fantasizing about young Mr. Forester, she'd never hear the end of it. "Jubilee. They make better mojitos." Sylvia forced a smile, pushing thoughts of Dale aside, but it was like pushing a carton of rocks up a hill with one hand. She couldn't do it. Her resolve to keep Dale at arm's length had already withered. If she could stop daydreaming about him for a minute, she'd realize the constant buzzing in her ears was an alarm bell telling her to take a step back. Far back—binocular back—and get a grip.

Chapter 15

The company jet began its descent, and Dale turned from his laptop and looked out the window. The view of the Manhattan skyline from ten thousand feet never failed to impress. The plane banked right, passed over the city, and then across the Hudson, heading for a private airfield on the Jersey side.

Dale took in a deep breath. He'd stayed longer in Buffalo than he'd planned, uncovering problems he hadn't quite figured out how to solve. Something wasn't right, of that he was certain. But he didn't have enough to go on. For now, he'd sleep on it and work it out with his executive planners tomorrow.

With the runway in view, thoughts of the Buffalo project began to recede and were replaced with his favorite subject, Sylvia Ramirez. Dale smiled for the first time in a week, and his shoulders relaxed. He wondered where she was tonight and what she was doing.

As the wheels hit the tarmac, his phone chimed, pulling him out of his reverie. He looked at the screen and found a text from his mother.

—Call me. Urgent.—

Dale swiped to his favorites and pressed *call*.

His mother answered in half a ring.

"Hey, what's wrong? Are you okay?"

"I'm fine. But I think there's going to be trouble,"

Candace said.

He wasn't in the mood for talking in code. "Can you be more specific? What kind of trouble?"

"I'm not sure exactly what is going on." Candace's voice sounded strained. "I have our attorneys looking into it as we speak. A reporter from *New Day Magazine* was sniffing around, asking me and several of the other board members questions about the Buffalo project."

Dale gripped his phone tighter. "What kind of questions?"

"He asked if I knew the names of the project's suppliers. He seemed particularly interested in who is supplying the cement for the buildings."

"What kind of crazy question is that? What did you say?" Dale held his breath.

"I said I didn't know and politely hung up. But that didn't stop him. He was outside the office today to get employees to go on record, asking them the same questions."

"Great, just great." Dale clenched a fist and tried to keep the exasperation out of his voice. "What do they know that we don't?"

New Day Magazine was one of the biggest gossip rags in print. Their headlines screamed from supermarket checkouts across the country. It didn't matter if the articles were true or completely fabricated, because people tended to believe headlines. While most magazines were dying, *New Day*'s sales were out the roof. They could afford to keep an entire legal team on retainer to handle the dozens of defamation suits thrown at them every month. Sadly, no one remembered if the victim of a story had been vindicated; all the public remembered were the accusations, even if they had been proven false.

Dale rubbed his forehead. "What do our attorneys say?"

"So far, nothing," Candace Forester said.

He blew out a long breath. "Something's terribly wrong. I'm going to bring Goff in on this." Having been with Forester for over fifteen years, Leonard Goff was the company's private investigator. As a retired veteran of the NYPD, he not only knew every corner of the city, but he also knew who to ask to get the right answers.

"Great idea, dear. Call me when you know anything more."

Ending the call, he looked out at the overcast night sky. The thought of another potentially damning article had the beginnings of a headache forming behind his eyes. He was trying to turn the company around and being blindsided like this was the last thing he needed. Swiping open his phone again, he called Leonard Goff. For now, it was all he could do.

His plane landed, and instead of heading straight to his apartment, he directed his driver to take him to uptown Manhattan. Checking his watch, he leaned back against the plush leather and sighed. He'd convinced himself he wasn't going uptown just to see her. The hour was late, and Sylvia had likely gone home. But he'd made the decision to go anyway, to check on the progress of the demolition. He stared out the window. Who was he kidding? It was ten o'clock, but he hoped she'd miraculously still be working. He hadn't stopped thinking about her the entire week he'd been away.

They'd communicated by text, email, and phone several times a day, all under the guise of discussing the plans and proposals for the new center. But he found himself looking forward to hearing her voice each day. He wanted to know how things were going in the neighborhood, and Sylvia had been eager to share the news, as well as the changes and additions she was working on with his chief architect, Marion.

The black SUV finally pulled up to the trailers, which were now serving as construction offices.

Dale pushed a button on a panel in the door frame, and his window slid down silently. Despite everything, he smiled as he stared at the enormous hole in the ground where the ramshackle old community center once stood. After all these years in the development game, it still amazed him a building could be totally destroyed, with the promise of something better being erected in its place. And in this case, a structure that would help more people.

He turned and looked out the other window. In the time he'd been gone, a chain link fence had been erected, surrounding a dozen work trailers. All were dark except one. "I'll be right back," he told his driver. He stepped out into the humid July night and walked toward the entrance.

"You looking for something, mister?" A tall burly man in a dark-green uniform stood in front of the gate, blocking the entrance with his body.

"I'd like to take a look around," Dale said.

The guard's expression was neutral.

"It's okay. You can let me in, I'm Dale Forester."

The guard registered no sign of recognition. "Let's see your ID, sir." The guard held out one hand while shining a flashlight in Dale's face with the other.

Dale stepped back and shielded his eyes. He gave a

little huff and was about to argue when he saw another guard heading toward him from down the block. He decided it would be easier to produce the ID than to cause a scene. He realized Sylvia had been right—not everyone recognized his face. To be treated like an ordinary person was an odd feeling, but all the same, he thought he could get used to the sensation.

"Sir?" The guard took a step toward him.

Dale gave a wry smile, reached inside his suit pocket, and took out his wallet. He pulled his driver's license out of the plastic sleeve and handed it over. "Here you go."

The guard took a few seconds to study it, then tilted his head to the Forester Industries sign hanging on the fence behind him. "You're *that* Forester?"

"Yup, that's me," Dale said. "What's your name?"

"Terrance Milton."

"You're doing a nice job, Terrance. May I go in now?"

The guard handed back his ID, opened the gate, and stepped aside.

Dale nodded, passed through the gate, and took the path on the right. When he reached the trailer, he barked out a laugh. Taped to the door was a makeshift sign that read—*NEIGHBORHOOD DREAM TEAM.* Taking the four aluminum steps in two long strides, he knocked on the door, but no one answered. He knocked again but still got no response. He jiggled the door handle and found it unlocked, so he stepped inside.

The front half of the trailer was in semi-darkness, but he could still make out a conference room of sorts, with a folding card table surrounded by four folding chairs. He turned left and took a few steps into a narrow galley way with a sink on one side and a small fridge and coffeemaker on the other.

At the back of the trailer, in a room serving as her office, he found Sylvia fast asleep—her head resting on the computer keyboard. He stopped, leaned against the doorway and stared, utterly dumbstruck by her beauty. Her skin glowed in the lamplight. Her lips were full and sensual. All thoughts vanished except how much he wanted to kiss her.

Sylvia must have sensed his presence because she opened her eyes and abruptly pushed away from the desk.

He smiled. “Hey, there.”

“Dale?” Her voice was hoarse. “Jeez, you nearly scared the life out of me.”

His smile widened, and he took a step forward.

Sylvia raised a hand. “Wait. What are you doing here? What time is it?” She wiped her mouth with the back of her hand. “And…how long have you been standing there?”

Dale shrugged. “I was in the neighborhood, it’s a little after ten o’clock, and I’ve been standing here for, oh”—he slid his shirt sleeve back and looked at this watch—“about four minutes. Does that answer all your questions?”

“Not exactly. The part about being in the neighborhood”—she stretched her arms overhead and yawned—“that part is lame.” Sylvia slumped back in her chair. “There’s no other word for it. It’s after ten at night, and we both know 181st Street is not your usual hangout.”

“But it will be.” A slow smile crossed his face. He expected her to respond, but she simply stared. “Okay,

okay. I got back from Buffalo, and I had an inexplicable urge to see the place…well, to see you. But I never expected you'd still be working."

Sylvia tugged at the edges of her T-shirt and pushed her hair out of her face. "Stalk much?" She put a hand over her mouth. "Sorry, I didn't mean it like that. You were staring, and I'm not a pretty sleeper. Mouth open. Drool. You know what I mean?"

"I didn't want to wake you. I was afraid I'd scare you."

"Well, mission un-accomplished." Sylvia smirked.

"I'm merely trying to get to know the neighborhood at all hours of the day and night."

Sylvia narrowed her gaze. "Why am I not buying that story?"

Dale ignored her question. "Since I'm here, and you're awake, how 'bout we go for a drink?"

"Ha! Right. At this time of night? This isn't lower Manhattan where you can get a cheeseburger and a glass of merlot at any hour of the day or night. This is the Heights, it's a respectable neighborhood, and they close it all down about this time. The only places open are a couple of all-night diners near the hospital."

"Okay, then let's get a coffee."

Sylvia tilted her head and looked up, her eyes narrowed.

The look on her face signaled she was weighing her options. But, Dale wasn't in the mood for a lengthy deliberation. Taking matters into his own hands, he was at her desk in three quick steps, lifting her out of her chair by her elbows until her face was inches from his. Dale's gaze drifted toward her full, luscious lips. He wanted to kiss her, and so he leaned closer, lost in the beauty of Sylvia Ramirez, and not caring if he ever found his way back.

Chapter 16

Sylvia's heart thumped against her chest as if it were trying to escape. She looked up into Dale's sea-green eyes framed by long, dark lashes and sighed. They reminded her of a tropical ocean, and she wanted to dive in. She imagined raising herself on the tips of her toes and kissing him. But the sirens going off in the back of her mind, telling her to steer clear, were getting louder and louder. Sylvia didn't want to listen to the alarm bells and turned off her inner chatter. *To hell with the warning bells*. Lifting her heels off the ground, she leaned toward Dale. She closed her eyes, ready to be consumed when the office phone rang. Startled, Sylvia stepped back and checked the caller ID. "I have to answer this. It's Security."

Dale looked at his watch. "At this hour?"

Sylvia held up her finger to silence Dale and answered the phone. "Hi, this is Sylvia. Uh-huh. Yup, leaving now. Thanks."

Dale tilted his head and raised an eyebrow.

"They call if I'm still here to tell me they're changing shifts. I guess the guys look out for me."

"Good to know." Dale smiled and took a step toward her.

Sylvia took a step back. The interruption had given her just enough time to come to her senses. Clearly, Dale hadn't gotten the message because he inched even closer.

Sylvia leaned back. *What's he thinking? Doesn't he know this has mistake written all over it in indelible neon ink?* She had to put a stop to whatever was happening between them. The obstacles were too numerous to count, but she ticked them off in her head as a reminder. *They worked together. He was rich. She wasn't. They traveled in different universes.* Lowering her gaze, she let her shoulders drop with the realization they had no future together. She busied herself with shutting down her computer and straightening the papers on her desk. Dale didn't move, forcing her to work around him.

"So, about that coffee?" Dale said. "Or maybe if you're hungry, we could grab a bite? Whichever you prefer."

Sylvia continued to straighten the already neat piles on her desk. Maybe if she ignored the invitation, he would drop it. She needed to maintain her resolve and keep Dale at arm's length.

"Look, I'm dying to hear about the plans you've been working on. Sylvia, I promise I'll only keep you out for half an hour."

"Okay." Sylvia quickly dropped her gaze to the floor. The word had flown out of her mouth, as if her body had been possessed by a lovesick teenager. That steely determination she'd promised herself had lasted a quarter of a second. Where Dale was concerned, she'd become a pushover.

****

Sylvia pulled open the door of her favorite diner, located on the corner of 169th and Broadway. The typical, late-night crowd, featuring hospital workers dressed in scrubs or white lab coats, seated on the swivel stools at the luncheon counter or scattered among the green leather booths lining the right wall.

A bald man behind the cash register called out for them to take a seat anywhere.

Sylvia chose a booth behind a couple and their young teenage son, sporting what looked like a new cast on his arm and drinking an ice-cream soda. Sylvia slid into the booth and reached for two large, much-used, laminated menus in the holder. “Here you go.”

Dale’s eyes widened. “There must be a hundred choices here.” He flipped through the stiff menu pages.

“Yeah. Aren’t New York diners the best?” Sylvia snorted a laugh.

Dale tilted his head. “Is this another one of your foodie hideaways?”

Sylvia thought for a moment and shrugged. “If you’ve got a craving for a burger or any kind of deli sandwich, and it’s midnight, this is the place to come.”

“Noted.” Dale continued to peruse his menu.

Sylvia pursed her lips and studied him. With all his money, he’d led a sheltered life. How could he not, when his life was filled with chauffeured cars, yacht clubs, and society parties? “Can I ask you a question?”

“Of course.” Dale didn’t look up.

Sylvia furrowed her brow. “Is this your first time in a diner?”

Dale’s gaze shifted up and to the left, as if he were thinking.

“Um, as a matter of fact, it is.”

Sylvia snorted and rolled her eyes.

“What? Why the attitude?”

“I mean, Dale, eating at a diner is such a New

York-y thing to do. You know, milkshakes and greasy fries. There must be several hundred, if not thousands of them, across all five Boroughs. There's even a reality show on the subject."

Dale shrugged.

"Boy, have you been missing out." Sylvia hoped her sarcasm hadn't gone unnoticed.

A bored-looking server stepped up to their booth, pad in hand, and slipped a pencil from behind his ear. "You ready?"

Sylvia nodded. "I'll have a BLT on rye, hold the mayo, extra-crispy fries, and a glass of iced tea, sweetened."

The server turned his attention to Dale.

"That sounds great. I'll have the same thing, but bring on the mayo," Dale said.

"You got it." The server placed the pencil back behind his ear, put the order pad in his front pocket, and slouched away.

Sylvia sat back, tucked her hair behind her ears, and looked around. With their order placed, she wasn't sure what to talk about next. The residual tension from their almost-kiss made her self-conscious. She plucked a napkin from the napkin holder and folded it in half and then in half again. She pressed down on the creases with laser-like concentration, searching for a neutral topic to talk about.

"So, I heard you got the kitchen set up at the Armory," Dale said.

Grateful for the conversation starter, Sylvia smiled. "Yes, and it's such a relief. We're finally back to serving food to the kids and senior citizens." Providing meals had been a larger hurdle than Sylvia had bargained for, and finally getting the kitchen and dining area up and running had been a weight off her shoulders. "Oh, and I met with your chief architect, Marion. Boy, is she amazing."

Dale nodded. "What she doesn't know about building buildings, well, it's not worth knowing."

Sylvia continued pressing against the crease of the paper napkin, not looking up. "You know, I was a little freaked out to meet her the first time."

"Really?" Dale leaned in. "Why?"

"First of all, she's your chief architect. Secondly, her reputation is like, I mean, she was listed as one of forty women under forty to watch this year, so, yeah, I was a little intimidated. I was afraid my ideas would be, you know, disregarded." Sylvia laughed self-consciously. "But, it was actually the complete opposite. Marion listened, took my ideas, and made them better."

"I'm glad it's working out. Marion *is* one of the best in the business." Dale tapped a finger on the table for emphasis. "We're lucky to have her." He sat back and continued. "She sent over the prints and specs for what you worked on. Looks like you've figured out how to utilize the space we gave you. There doesn't seem to be a wasted square foot."

"That was the idea. Make the most of what we've got." Sylvia blew on her fingers and made a polishing motion on her sleeve. "But we're not quite finished. That's what I was working on tonight before I fell asleep and drooled all over the keyboard."

They both laughed.

"Are you almost finished?" Dale asked.

"Almost, but I need to talk to your IT people about

a couple of things. I want to put in a state-of-the-art computer science room, with at least thirty or forty computers, so I need to make sure we can connect them all without slowing down our Internet, or worse, having to share it with the other tenants in the building."

"Where are you planning to get the money for all this?" Dale frowned. "I mean, I don't want to rain on your parade, but…that's ambitious."

"No worries, rain away. I got a big umbrella."

Dale laughed.

"I'm glad you think this is amusing, but you forget, I'm the queen of fundraising. Once I have the plans approved, I'll start working on bringing in the bucks. Don't you worry. I'll get those computers in there." Sylvia paused. "Unless Forester Industries would like to donate all of them?" She batted her eyelashes and put on a serene smile.

"Well, I'm sure we're good for at least five. But they would be from me personally. Forester has put a sizable chunk of change into re-designing the plans and building for the new community center. And there are other organizations and charities we're pledged to help as well."

Sylvia gave a small pout. "Well, first, thanks for the computer donation. And second, don't feel bad; it might be hard for me to admit, but Forester Industries is really coming through for us. And it has not gone unnoticed."

"Wait, let me see if I get this straight"—Dale sat forward, a smirk on his face—"are you *thanking* us?"

The server arrived and placed their plates on the table. "Anything else I can get you?"

"No, thanks," they both said at the same time, then

simultaneously reached for the saltshaker.

"After you," Dale said.

"Thanks." Sylvia took her time salting her fries. "Uh, yeah…I'm thanking you." She picked up a fry and bit into it, slowly chewing and staring at Dale, who was once again wearing that sly smile of his. "Don't get cocky"— she pointed her half-eaten fry at him—"it's a thank you, not a tribute in *The Times*."

Dale let out a deep, spontaneous laugh. "I'll try to keep that in mind."

Sylvia took out her phone and began typing.

"Uh, are you sending a text at this time of night?"

"Nope." Sylvia didn't look up. "I'm making a list of potential donors. I'm thinking of asking for television monitors, too. It would be amazing if we could create a media center for the kids. There's a group who hang out together and shoot movies on their phones. They should have a place to collaborate and edit their work. Who knows, maybe one of them is the next award-winning filmmaker just waiting for the right tools to make a great film." She typed one final thought before putting away her phone. "Sorry, sometimes these things take longer than I'd like… What? Again with the staring?" She grabbed a paper napkin from the dispenser. "Do I have food on my face?"

"No."

"Then what are you looking at?"

"I was thinking…" Dale cocked his head but didn't continue his thought.

Sylvia huffed. "Well, if you're not going to tell me what you were thinking, I'll continue eating." She took a bite of her sandwich and waited for him to say what was on his mind, but he continued watching her in silence. "Come on, seriously. What's in that head of yours?"

"All your talk about donations—"

"Please"—Sylvia put up a hand—"I know I've got a lot of work to do to raise the kind of funds I'm talking about."

"That's just it. I have an idea on how you might get all the money you need in one night." Dale gave a toothy grin.

"Unless it's robbing a bank or winning the lottery, I'm not following you."

"The Starlight Ball is in four weeks." Dale sat taller, his tone triumphant.

"Oh, please, don't remind me." Sylvia sank back against the faux leather.

"Why do say it with such dread?"

"Because I spent the better part of two years trying to get them to recognize our community center as a viable organization so it could qualify for their donations. But no, they would only sponsor national groups. Which to my way of thinking is absurd because…well, why not make the city you live in a better place? It makes no sense." Sylvia shook her head. "So, as far as I'm concerned, those people are not only so rich they need to *give* their money away, they're also silly, uncaring idiots who can't see a great cause when it's in their own backyard."

"Wow, don't hold back. Please tell me how you really feel."

"No, seriously, that charity event is dead to me." Sylvia crumpled up her napkin and reached for another in the dispenser.

"Wait a minute. Not so fast. What if you could

go?"

Sylvia scoffed. "Yeah, right. As what? The help?"

"No. As my date."

The other sounds in the diner were suddenly audible. Sylvia could clearly hear forks scraping against plates and the sizzle of burgers frying on the grill. She gulped. She didn't know what she was reacting to: being on a date with this impossibly handsome man, or going to one of New York City's biggest annual charity events, or the possibility of securing all the money she needed in one evening. Probably all of it. "Are you seriously asking me?"

"I am, yes. I'll introduce you to the people you need to know. The ones who can write a hundred-thousand-dollar check without a second thought."

Sylvia played with her fork and took a moment to consider what Dale had offered. The corners of her lips turned up in a slow smile, as she imagined an evening surrounded by people who had nothing to do but give away their money. It was like winning the lottery. She let out a throaty laugh and clapped her hands. "That would be so amazing. I could raise money for computers and the Girls Up program at the same time. This is too exciting!"

"So, is that a, yes?"

"Yes. Yes. Yes!" Sylvia spoke loud enough for several of their fellow diners to stare. Ignoring them, she dug into her fries. This was turning out to be one of the best days she'd had in a long time. But the question in the back of her mind gave her pause. Was this a date?

Chapter 17

"Would you stop making such a big deal out of this?" Sylvia stamped a foot on the pavement in the middle of the crosswalk on Fourteenth Street.

"Do. Not. Do. This." Randi put a hand on her hip. "Girl, I'm your best friend. If I can't tell you, who will?"

"*Ay, la dramatica!*" Sylvia waved a hand dismissively. "You always have to act like the end of the world is coming. It's just a charity ball."

"I'm sorry if my mind hasn't had a chance to catch up with *your* reality." Randi's voice rose an octave, as dozens of pedestrians passed them on the crowded street. "Because I can't freaking believe this is happening."

Sylvia leaned in. "People are legit staring. You wanna take it down a notch?" Traffic had started to move again, and cars were honking all around them. She steered Randi up onto the sidewalk.

"It's not like giving him a personal tour of the neighborhood wasn't enough." Randi threw up her hands. "Now you're going on a date. Like for real? And do you know how ridiculous the word *ball* sounds? Who are you, Cinder-freaking-ella? Who goes to *balls*?"

Sylvia stiffened. "Randi, you're making too much of this."

"No. I'm not. In fact, you're not making enough of it. First, you tell me you're taking me to lunch. You act all mysterious when I ask what's the special occasion? And you tell me you have a date, and you want me to help you shop. So, I'm thinking, finally, Sylvia's met a guy. At last, she's over Julian. Let's go to lunch, celebrate, and then we'll pick out a dress that will make this guy, whoever he is, salivate. But n-o-o-o-o-o-o-o." Randi's eyes widened. And then widened an inch more. "That's not it at all. Your so-called date is none other than…wait for it…Dale-our-boss-who-is-richer-than-Midas-Forester." She put her hands on her hips. "Are you for real?"

Pedestrians continued to walk around them, as if they didn't even notice two best friends in a heated argument in the middle of the sidewalk. "I do not understand why you hate him so much." Sylvia gripped the strap of her purse.

"I don't hate him in general. I only hate him for you. Look, I'm finally willing to admit he's doing good things for the community. I'll even go so far as to say I appreciate he put us on his payroll, but that's as far as it goes. You and I, we're not in his league. And in the end, he'll hurt you." Randi paused and glared. "Have you forgotten Julian and what he put you through?"

"No," Sylvia snapped. "I have not forgotten. My memory is in perfect working order. Thank you very much."

"Don't raise your eyebrows at me," Randi said. "My feelings happen to be right ninety-nine percent of the time. I could have been a psychic if I'd wanted to. Anyway, I can smell trouble coming. And it's rank. You're going to get hurt. I feel it in my bones. I don't want it to be true. I'm just saying."

"All right, enough. Let's go." Beckoning Randi with her hand, Sylvia began walking. "You've made it abundantly clear how you feel. I get it. But this ball gives us the opportunity to raise some serious cash for the center and Girls Up, and I'm not gonna miss the chance." She stopped at the store entrance and turned, only to find she'd left Randi standing on the street corner twenty feet away.

Grabbing the door handle with one hand, she snapped her fingers with the other. "Come on." Sylvia narrowed her gaze and raised an eyebrow as she held the door open.

Randi sauntered past.

Holding onto the scream she wanted to let out, Sylvia marched straight toward the evening gowns at the back of the outlet store.

For several minutes, she searched the racks in silence. Except for the staccato clacking of hangers forcefully being slid from one dress to the next, no one except Sylvia would have known Randi was annoyed. She needed to smooth this over and try to somehow salvage the day. "Look"—Sylvia let out a heavy sigh—"this is an opportunity for the community center. It doesn't get any simpler than that. Can we try and enjoy an afternoon?"

"Fine." Randi leaned on the rack. "But, girl, just so we're clear, I'm here under protest and only to make sure you don't buy a dress that'll embarrass you. Seems like all I do since we hooked up with this guy is sit around, watching *you* try on clothes."

Sylvia chose to ignore Randi's last comment and concentrated on finding a dress that would jump up and scream—*Buy me. I will make your body look like it was meant to be worshipped.* "Ooh, what do we have here?" She held up a purple, off-the-shoulder silk dress and placed it against her torso. "What do you think?"

"Ew, that color clashes with your skin tone." Randi made a gagging motion. "Tell it no and put it away."

Sylvia pursed her lips, shook her head, and then shoved it back into the overcrowded rack.

"Tell me, what exactly is your plan at this ball?" Randi asked. "You're just gonna go up to some rich dude and ask for twenty thou? As if they carry their checkbooks with them. That's what they have bankers for. The only time these people actually touch their money is when they're throwing a dollar tip to the valet."

Sylvia flinched. Randi had hit a nerve, because Sylvia didn't have a specific plan. She'd been so excited to be invited that she was counting on Dale to make the introductions. She hadn't thought beyond that. But she'd rather die than tell Randi she was trusting Dale to get them what they needed. Instead, she thumped a hand on top of the rack. "*Ay*, this is what we've always *wanted*. To be close to the power source. You wanna spend the rest of this afternoon going over the same ground? Because it's getting exhausting. Can't we just have a little fun? You know—like we used to?"

Randi grunted, continuing to slide one hanger after another on the rack.

When she looked up, Sylvia saw the tiniest lift at the corner of her mouth. "Ha! See, you can't stay mad at me."

Randi relented. "Okay, okay. I'll give it a rest. But let's be clear, I'm not putting this to bed permanently—

only for this afternoon."

"Better than nothing." Sylvia shrugged, and they spent the next ten minutes pulling dresses off the racks.

"Here's another one. You'll look amazing in it." Randi handed Sylvia a strapless, floor-length, deep-blue satin gown. "I think you've got enough. Time for you to try these on."

Sylvia grabbed the gown and headed toward the dressing rooms. She checked in with a harried-looking attendant, who counted the gowns and handed her a plastic door card with the number seven.

"Oh, and those, too." Sylvia tilted her head toward Randi's dress-laden arms.

The attendant frowned. "You know you can't be in the same dressing room."

"Yeah, yeah. Okay," Randi said. "I have six."

The attendant counted them anyway and, once satisfied, handed Randi a similar card with the number six. "The last two dressing rooms in the back are free."

Sylvia nodded and headed toward the back. She pushed aside the vinyl curtain of her room and hung her haul on the hook. Staring at herself in the mirror, she pushed her hair off her face, and put a hand on a hip, and narrowed her eyes. "Okay, girl. You need to look fabulous." Turning, she reached for the deep-blue satin, floor-length gown.

Minutes later, Randi crossed the aisle into Sylvia's dressing room, hung up the six dresses, sank to the floor, and crossed her arms over her knees. "All right. Let's see what you got."

Five dresses into what had now become a fashion show, Sylvia slipped on a beaded, lace front gown.

"That's cute." Randi tilted her head from side to

side. "Yeah, I like it."

Sylvia stood sideways, inspecting herself from all angles in the three-way mirror. "Nah." She shook her head. "White is tricky on me. Makes my butt look huge."

"It is not. You're curvy in all the right places," Randi said.

"I wonder if Dale would like it." Sylvia turned and inspected herself in the mirror once more before realizing what she'd said. She clasped a hand over her mouth. "Oh, shoot. Did I say that out loud?"

On cue, Randi pounced. "I knew it. You like him! See, that look right there says it all. Gurl, you're in deep, and you got it bad."

Sylvia reached for a champagne-colored tulle gown on the hook behind her and threw it at Randi.

"Hey, watch it." Randi pulled the dress off her head. "We break it. We have to buy it."

"Okay. I admit it. I like him. I shouldn't. But I do. Satisfied?"

Randi jumped up and put the dress in the growing, not-ever-going-to-wear pile. "You know if there were a wrong side of things, this is on the far side of that." She threw her hands up. "Just saying."

"I know. But don't worry. It's a no thing. Really. Besides, we are *so* not right for each other. I mean, it's not like I can forget he's richer than King Midas."

"Yeah, not a thing one could easily get amnesia about." Randi crossed her arms over her chest. "Look. You know how I feel. But you're a big girl, and there isn't much I can say or do that's gonna stop you from the collision course you're on."

"Oh, Randi. Don't be like that." Sylvia put a hand

on Randi's shoulder. "I have no idea what I'm doing here. But I am trying to be cautious. And my heart is in the right place. Regardless of what I feel for Dale, I am trying to get what we need for the community center and for Girls Up."

Sighing, Randi gave a half smile. "As much as I complain and harass you, I know your heart is in the right place. I just hope he doesn't stomp on it."

The idea of suffering another heartbreak wasn't something Sylvia would be able to endure. Not again. Despite her growing feelings for Dale, Randi was right. But she had no idea how to slow the express train to disaster she seemed to be riding.

"Look, I'm only saying, however it goes, I'll be here for you."

Sylvia wrapped her arms around Randi and hugged her. "You're the best," she whispered in Randi's ear.

"Okay, that's enough." Randi pushed Sylvia away and lifted a dress from a hook on the wall. "You're buying this one." She held out a red, boat-neck, silk jersey gown with a plunging V in the back. "This one says it all. I mean, if you're going out there to represent the center, you need to look amazing."

Sylvia's face lit up. "It is fabulous, isn't it?"

"Yup." Randi scooped up the pile of discarded dresses and pulled back the dressing room curtain. She handed the rejects to the dressing room clerk.

Once outside, Sylvia and Randi proceeded to the back of the line at the register.

"You know, all this shopping has made me hungry, and you promised me lunch. Today I'm in the mood for something with calories in the triple digits," Randi said.

Inching up toward the head of the line, Sylvia

furrowed her brow. "I thought we were having salads because you're on a diet."

"Yeah. That was yesterday." Randi snorted. "You know, I did some calculating, and in the past five years, I've lost over 200 pounds."

Sylvia stopped dead in her tracks. "You didn't have 200 pounds to lose. What are you talking about?"

"No. I didn't. But, I keep losing the same five pounds over, and over, and over again. It adds up."

"All right"—Sylvia chuckled—"let's get something sinful. How 'bout the place on University Street? The one with triple-decker burgers on the menu." She handed her dress to the cashier. "But I can't take long. I've got to get to work."

"Work?" Randi's brow creased. "It's Saturday. We're off. Remember?"

"I know, but I need to make a few tiny changes to the proposal." Sylvia held her thumb and forefinger an inch apart.

"The proposal is perfect." Randi sucked in a breath. "This crush thing you have on Dale is clouding your ability to see your own brilliance. Hit *send* already."

The machine card reader beeped, displaying the total. Sylvia swiped her credit card and signed with the plastic stylus. As far as the proposal was concerned, she was relieved to know in her heart she wasn't putting in the extra hours because she wanted Dale to like her. It was about getting the proposal perfect. It had to be because the entire community was counting on her. She turned to face Randi. "Don't worry. It won't take me long."

The cashier handed Sylvia her receipt and her dress

wrapped in a garment bag.

"Thank you." Sylvia smiled.

Randi looked up at her. "Jeez. You're impossible. Seems like nothing I say is gonna change your mind. You're going to go back to the office."

"Now you're catching on." Sylvia put one arm around Randi and pulled her close.

Randi shrugged. "Whatever. You know I'll always be there for you."

Sylvia barked out a throaty laugh. "Yup. It's ride-or-die, girl, ride-or-die."

****

Her favorite Latin band was playing in the background for several seconds before Sylvia realized it was her ringtone for Randi. In a daze, she grabbed her phone and swiped it open. "Hello?"

"Do not tell me you are still working?"

Randi's voice came through loud, puncturing the silence in the trailer. Sylvia jerked upright. "Oh, no. What time is it?"

"Seriously? It's a little past midnight, and I was worried. You didn't answer any of my texts. What are you doing, rewriting the Constitution?"

Wiping dribble from her chin, she looked around. "Gosh, I think I fell asleep on my keyboard again." Silence came from the other end. "Randi? Hello? Can you hear me?"

"Oh, I hear you loud and freakin' clear. I was too busy being annoyed to speak. Now, you listen to me. Go home. The proposal was already great. Stop fussing, okay? You don't need to impress Dale Forester."

Her stomach clenched. "I'm not—"

"I'm gonna stop you right there. We both know

that's exactly what you were doing."

With a groan, Sylvia put her forehead on the desk. "Randi, please let's not rewind the same conversation we had this afternoon."

"Don't Randi me. What I'm saying is you've already proven your worth. Forester Industries can't do this project without you, so you don't need to kill yourself because you're crushing on Mr. Richie Rich."

"Are you done?" Sylvia lifted her chin and rolled her eyes toward the ceiling.

"*Chica*, you don't need to get snotty. I care about you. I don't want you to be hurt."

Sylvia slumped back in her chair and pushed her hair away from her eyes. "I know. I love you, too. And you're right, but can we talk about this in the morning?"

"Sure, as long as you promise me you're going home right now."

The insistence in Randi's voice propelled Sylvia out of her chair. "I swear. I'm leaving."

"I'm gonna stay on the phone until I hear the trailer door shut."

"That's really not necessary." She scanned the marked-up pages of her proposal strewn across the desk.

"Start walkin'. I'll wait."

Sylvia huffed. "Did you hear that? I'm huffing because now *you're* annoying the life out of me."

"Since your *boyfriend* isn't there to escort you, someone needs to make sure you get home safely."

"Okay, *mami*. I'm putting away my papers now. And he's not my boyfriend." She was grateful Randi wasn't there to see the flush she felt working its way up her cheeks.

"Great. I'll sing while you wrap it up."

Sylvia put her phone on the desk and pressed the Speaker button. She could hear Randi singing their favorite song a cappella. "You never could carry a tune."

Randi chuckled. "Yeah, but I got great rhythm."

"Ha!" Sylvia laughed and began to sing along with Randi, doing a little salsa twirl around her desk as she packed up. After stacking her papers in a neat pile, she hit Save on her project and shut down her computer. Grabbing her phone and taking it off Speaker, she held it between her ear and shoulder, picked up her purse, and turned off the desk lamp. "I'm heading toward the door now."

"*¡Finalmente!* I need my beauty rest, too," Randi said. "We got a meeting first thing in the morning—"

"I know, I know. And you're flying out tomorrow afternoon to Puerto Rico. I wish I was go—*Aaaaggggghhhhh!*"

Chapter 18

Sylvia's eyes blinked open to harsh overhead lights. The sound of rhythmic beeping was piercing, and the smell of antiseptic hung heavy in the air. Shading her eyes with a hand, she searched her surroundings, but the images wouldn't come into focus. "Hello?" Her throat was dry, and her voice was barely above a whisper.

"Take it easy. Don't try to sit up."

Through the haze, the voice sounded familiar. "Dale, is that you?" If it weren't for the intense pain in her body, she would have thought she was dreaming. "What happened? Where am I?"

"You fell." Dale stepped forward and gripped the front railing of the bed. "You're in the hospital."

"The hospital?" The last thing she remembered was talking to Randi and leaving the trailer. "I don't understand. Where's Randi?"

"I'm right here." Randi stepped into the room. "Thank God. You're awake. I was just at the nurses' station. They say the doctor will be here any minute."

When Sylvia tried to sit up, she winced. "Randi, what's going on? My head is killing me."

"Honey, when you fell, you hit your head and possibly broke your ankle." Randi's frown came into focus as she stepped closer. "We're waiting for the x-rays."

"You're lucky it wasn't worse," Dale added.

"Did I miss a step?"

"No. It wasn't you," Randi said. "Looks like while you were in the trailer working, someone removed the aluminum staircase at the front door. So, instead of your foot landing on the first step, you fell five feet onto the dirt pathway."

Sylvia couldn't make sense of what Randi was saying. She took in a breath, and with it came a sharp pain in her shoulder blade. She squeezed her eyes shut, waiting for the sensation to subside.

"Are you okay?" Randi asked.

Sylvia barely nodded.

"Try and relax." Dale raked a hand through his hair and took a step back.

"I can't. I need answers. How did—" A sharp, shooting pain in her ankle seemed to take over her entire body, and Sylvia clenched her jaw.

Dale leaned in. "Sylvia, what's happening?"

Sucking in a deep breath, she opened her eyes and looked at him. "It's okay. What I want to know is how did you get here?" Her words came out in a pained whisper.

"The security guards called me."

Sylvia couldn't read Dale's expression. "Why would they call you?"

"I'm the CEO. I'm notified whenever there's a case of vandalism or an accident on Forester properties. It's my responsibility to respond and initiate an investigation."

"Oh." Sylvia waited for him to elaborate, but he didn't. She hoped his presence was more than merely a corporate responsibility. He stood at the foot of the bed, head down, hands in his pockets, saying nothing. Just as the moment was about to get awkward, his phone rang. The speed with which he pulled his phone out and excused himself to take the call gave her the answer. He was at the hospital because she was a problem that needed to be solved. She closed her eyes in disappointment.

Every part of her body felt as if it had been hurled out of a window. She leaned back against the pillow and tried to forget about the throbbing in her head and the searing pain in her right ankle. Sylvia felt shattered from the inside out—emotionally and physically.

The first and only time she'd ever been inside a hospital had been five years ago, when her mother lay dying. Since meeting Dale, she'd found herself in a hospital twice in one month. The irony wasn't lost on her. Even if she didn't believe in signs, this had *bad* written all over it. "When can I leave? I really want to go home now."

Randi moved closer and held her hand. "We need to wait for the—"

"Ah, good. You're awake. Hello, Ms. Ramirez. I'm Dr. Torres."

Sylvia raised her head and squinted toward the doorway. A tall woman with big brown eyes beneath a mass of curly gray hair walked in and stood at the foot of the bed. The doctor's warm smile had a soothing effect, and Sylvia relaxed the muscles in her face. "Doctor. When can I get out of here?"

Torres wrinkled her brow. "I can understand you being anxious to get home, but we'd like to keep you here overnight—for observation."

"No, I can't." The words came out in a rush. She

shuddered, remembering the bill Miguel received from his two-day stint. While she did have health insurance, the only policy she could afford had minimal coverage, and she'd still be on the hook for the ten-thousand-dollar deductible. "I really need to go."

"Ms. Ramirez, I get it. No one likes staying in the hospital, but you took a bad fall. You were unconscious for over an hour. We want to rule out any possibility of a concussion and make sure there's no internal bleeding." The doctor paused and then brightened. "There is good news, though. Initially, we thought you might have broken your ankle because of the swelling and discoloration. But the x-rays show no fracture. However, there is a tear in one of the ligaments, and you've suffered a very bad sprain."

Sylvia gave a weak smile. "No wonder it hurts."

The doctor took a step closer. "We can give you something stronger for the pain, if you like."

"No. Thanks." Unless Sylvia was in mortal anguish, she rarely even took aspirin. The last thing she needed or wanted was to become reliant on pain medication. She'd rather tough it out.

Dr. Torres nodded. "Okay, then. We'll have a nurse in here shortly to set your ankle in a boot and give you a pair of crutches. The social worker will be by in the morning to make sure you have someone who can help you get around at home." She stepped in front of the computer console stationed at the side of the bed and began typing. "I'm making a few notes in your chart for the nurse."

Sylvia stared at the doctor, not certain she'd heard her correctly. "Why would I need help?"

"Because you'll have to stay off your foot for at

least two weeks"—the doctor gave a one-shoulder shrug and continued typing—"maybe three, so the ankle heals properly." She looked up from the screen. "Do you have someone who can help?"

Sylvia's mouth went dry, and she began to experience a growing sense of panic. *Help me? Who?* Apart from Randi, she had no one, and Randi would be leaving for Puerto Rico tomorrow to help her mother move into a new condo. She inhaled deeply, trying to slow her heart rate. She hadn't felt this deep a sense of loneliness since the death of her mother.

"So, we all set here?" Dr. Torres put her hands inside the pockets of her white lab coat.

Sylvia nodded. What else could she do? She would have to figure out how to manage on her own.

"Then, if you have no other questions, I'll see you in a few hours." Dr. Torres smiled and left.

Gingerly turning her body to face the window, Sylvia clenched her fists and forced herself not to cry.

"Don't worry, *chica.* We got this," Randi said. "You can stay at my place while I'm in PR."

Sylvia looked at Randi. "I know you mean well, but that's not going to work. Your roommates would freak. They didn't sign up for unpaid home health care." Unable to stop the tears, Sylvia let them flow. Everything in her life seemed to be falling apart. First, the center, and now this. She needed time to think, but her mind was like a cloud wrapped inside a fog, and she couldn't focus. She turned toward the door as Dale stepped back into the room. She didn't want him to see her like this.

"What's happening?" Dale's concern was etched in the creases of his forehead.

Randi waved a dismissive hand. "It's nothing. Nothing you need to worry about."

Dale scratched the back of his neck. "I…I…I can't believe this happened on my property."

"*Hmmph.* Believe it." Randi sat on the edge of the bed and rubbed Sylvia's back. "*Pobrecita.* It's gonna be okay."

The soothing motion should have made Sylvia feel better, but all it did was bring out more tears.

"Awww, honey. Please don't cry." Randi reached for a tissue on the bedside table and handed it to Sylvia. "I'll call my roommates now. We'll figure this out."

"No, Randi"—Sylvia blew her nose—"I'll stay at my apartment."

"Don't be ridiculous. You live in a five-floor walkup. Delivery people won't climb those stairs, even if you give them a five-dollar tip."

"I can't stay at your place—four people using one bathroom is three too many." She wiped her tears with the back of her hand. "It's okay, really."

"Let me help." Dale moved closer.

"Didn't realize you were still here." Sylvia's words were harsh. She'd said them, intending to hurt Dale's feelings. The last thing she wanted was for him to think she cared about him when it was painfully obvious she'd become a business problem he needed to handle.

"Sorry, I want to help. I'm incredibly disturbed by what's happened," Dale said.

"You're incredibly disturbed?" Randi scoffed.

"Yes, I am." Dale stepped closer to the side of the bed. "Sylvia, I hate that you're hurt. I hate that someone did this. And you can believe I'm going to get to the bottom of it because—"

"Hey"—Randi shot him a death stare—"can we discuss this later?"

"What is it you're not telling me? Spill. Now." The effort it took to demand an answer left Sylvia's body shaking. And she was in no mood for this. Whatever this was. Her gaze went from Randi to Dale. "Please, tell me."

Several seconds passed before Dale spoke. "We're in the process of investigating what happened. We don't have enough information yet, but we're working on it."

"Other damages?" Sylvia asked.

Randi and Dale remained silent.

Their gazes shifted around the room, as if they were looking for something. "Seriously? Was nothing else disturbed?"

Randi shook her head.

Ignoring the pounding headache, she tried to focus and make sense of the situation. And then she remembered what Randi had said, the aluminum steps to the trailer were missing…heavy steps not easily moved on their own. They would have had to be physically moved from the door. But why would anyone *do* that? Someone had intentionally tried to hurt her. Bile rose in the back of her throat. "Who could hate me this much?"

"Awwww, girl." Randi took Sylvia's hands. "Don't think that way. Let the security team and the police do their thing. I'm sure it was just neighborhood vandals. They probably did it for a laugh."

"Not funny." She laid her head back against the pillow and stared at the blank television screen high up on the opposite wall. Shaken to her core, Sylvia's tears flowed down her cheeks again, and her body shook as she silently sobbed. *She'd been the target.*

The mattress sank slightly as Dale sat on the opposite side of the bed. "Sylvia, both the police and our in-house investigators are looking into this. We're going to find out who's responsible. In the meantime, until you're back on your feet, I want you to stay at my place."

The entire situation gave her a knot in the pit of her stomach, and Sylvia squeezed her eyes shut. Taking in a short breath, she turned and looked at Dale. "I can't stay with you."

"Of course, you can."

"No. She can't." Randi huffed.

Dale held up a hand. "Wait. Just listen to me, both of you."

"Absolutely not," Randi said.

"Please." Dale put up his other hand. "Let's all take a breath."

"Randi, let's hear what he has to say." Sylvia wanted more than anything to believe Dale's heart was in the right place.

"My apartment is fairly large." Dale paused. "Sylvia, you won't even have to see me, if you don't want to."

The knot in her stomach grew tighter. Those were not the words she'd wanted to hear.

"If she doesn't have to see you, as you say, who will take care of her?" Randi pursed her lips and stared.

"I have a staff."

"Of course, you do." Randi's lips tightened into a thin line.

Sylvia lay sandwiched between Randi and Dale.

She knew she should err on the side of caution and figure out how to make things work at Randi's crowded apartment. But her heart wouldn't give up. Maybe there was a chance she was more than a corporate liability. She wanted to believe Dale cared.

"You can stay as long as you need," Dale said. "I'll make sure you get to your doctor's appointments. When you're well enough, I can set up a work area. You can even conduct meetings via video conferencing. Please, Sylvia. It's the least I can do."

The least he could do? What happened to that almost-kiss? Did he really not care about her beyond the fact she was an employee? Was he worried she might sue the company? That had to be it. His lawyers probably told him to keep his distance and follow protocol. But if that were the case, why was he offering his apartment? She was hurt, angry, and confused. And the source of the confusion was sitting right in front of her.

The words *no, thanks* lodged in the back of her throat. But she couldn't speak. She wanted to be near Dale. It was easy to rationalize staying with him since Randi would be out of town, and her three roommates were iffy propositions. So, she looked down at the thin white hospital sheet and mumbled what she'd wanted to say all along. "All right, I accept your invitation." She hoped she wasn't making the second biggest mistake in her life. Her ex, Julian, being the first.

Chapter 19

The hospital's automatic doors slid open, and Dale pushed Sylvia's wheelchair out into the bright daylight toward the waiting SUV. The moment his driver opened the passenger door, Dale realized he should have chosen a different vehicle. Sylvia wouldn't be able to climb up into the back seat.

Instinctively, he felt Randi's eyes boring into the back of his head and turned to face her. Not wanting to go yet another round over his care-taking capabilities, he headed it off by scooping Sylvia up out of the wheelchair and into his arms. Her delicate face was inches from his. For a moment, he was motionless, enchanted by the color of her eyes. The green flecks in her irises seem to sparkle. Why had he never noticed before? As his gaze traveled down toward her lips, he thought he saw a tentative smile. It wasn't her full-on sunshine model, but definitely an improvement over the last few hours.

Ever since he'd arrived earlier that morning to make sure the hospital bill was charged to the company, she'd been distant. Hours had passed since he was first contacted by his security team, and he still couldn't wrap his mind around the fact that Sylvia had been a target. It scared him, and he'd been hyper-focused on the situation, calling his investigators every thirty minutes for an update. It hadn't helped that heavy rainfall in the early morning hours turned any footprints at the site into a muddy mess.

Randi interrupted his thoughts by pushing past him to stash Sylvia's crutches into the back of the vehicle. "Uh, Mr. Forester? Are you waiting for an invitation to put her down?"

Dale sighed and gave Randi a short nod. "Lower your head." He gently placed Sylvia onto the rear seat. A distinct feeling of what he could only describe as absence came over him when she removed her arms from around his neck. "You okay?"

"Yes. Fine."

The warmth of her sweet breath had him wondering if bringing her back to his apartment was the smartest idea. He'd told himself he couldn't bear the thought of Sylvia trying to manage on her own in a fifth-floor walk-up. But the truth was, he *wanted* to take care of her. If she'd told him she lived on the ground floor of an apartment building with a handicap ramp, he would still have insisted she stay with him. He wanted to be near her.

Randi nudged Dale aside. "Listen, Sylvia. For the last time, are you sure this is what you want?"

"I'll be fine. Now go before you miss your flight." She leaned toward Randi and kissed her on the cheek.

"I'm gonna call you tonight and check that you're being taken care of."

Dale clenched his fists. Deep down, he knew Randi was only trying to protect her best friend. What she failed to realize is they had the same intentions.

****

The drive downtown to Dale's apartment was relatively silent. Apart from Sylvia's yes or no answers regarding any dietary restrictions, she hadn't said another word.

When the car pulled up to his apartment on east Eighty-Fifth Street, Dale jumped out, jogged to the other side of the SUV, and opened Sylvia's door.

Two burly uniformed doormen descended the building's steps and began unloading the vehicle.

"Thanks, Tom," Dale said to the one nearest him. He lifted Sylvia out of the car and placed her in the wheelchair.

"Can I help you with that, sir?" Tom asked.

Dale shook his head. "Thanks, I've got her. Just make sure her bag and the crutches make it upstairs."

"Yes, sir."

Pushing the wheelchair into the front entrance, Dale proceeded through the main lobby and past two elevators. He made a sharp right turn. Yet another attendant pulled open a door leading to a small alcove with a single elevator and pressed a button on the outside panel.

While they waited, Dale tapped his foot on the shiny marble floor, filling the awkward silence that had surrounded them since they'd left the hospital. When the private car arrived, he pushed the chair inside and inserted a small key into an inset silver panel. The door slid silently closed.

"Very space age," Sylvia said. "What floor are we going to?"

"To the top," Dale said.

Sylvia looked up at him. "I should've guessed."

"Ms. Ramirez, do I detect a note of sarcasm in your voice?"

"Nope. That was just me talking and rolling my

eyes at the same time."

Dale chuckled. She was finally saying more than two words at a time. Even if they weren't complimentary, she was at least speaking.

"Are we moving?" Sylvia asked.

"Yes, this elevator is exceptionally quiet."

"No kidding. So, really, what floor are we going to?"

"Like I said, the top." He smiled, wanting to see the look on her face when she saw the view from his apartment because he did want to impress her. What Sylvia thought of him was important.

Moments later, the elevator door slid silently open, revealing a line of three people standing at attention in a large, airy foyer. "Sylvia, welcome to my home."

****

Sylvia tried to keep her jaw from hanging on its hinges. She wanted to phone Randi that minute and let her know any trepidation she'd felt about being left alone with Dale had been unnecessary.

Clearing his throat, Dale stepped to the side of the wheelchair. "Ms. Ramirez, this is Gretchen, the chef, and Mrs. Traylor, the housekeeper, and Marc Richards, my personal assistant."

All three nodded in her direction.

"It's nice to meet you." Sylvia had to force herself not to crack up laughing. Was this for real? She'd known Dale was wealthy, but this was beyond what she could think with. He was one man, for goodness sake. Who needed all this help?

Mrs. Traylor, a short, stocky woman, stepped forward. "If you require anything, Ms. Ramirez, please do not hesitate to ask."

"Please, call me Sylvia." The idea of anyone waiting on her was both intimidating and alarming. If anything, she wanted his staff to treat her as they would treat each other.

Their polite but tight-lipped smiles indicated that was never going to happen.

"I've arranged for Ms. Ramirez to take the rooms off the library, sir."

"Perfect, I'll take her there now. Thank you, Mrs. Traylor." Dale rested a hand on Sylvia's shoulder.

Her stomach flipped and then bottomed out. She didn't seem to be able to fight it. How could she? She was tired and in pain. Her nerves were frayed. The fact that her injuries stemmed from intentional harm still freaked her out. In less than twenty-four hours, she'd gone from dancing out of her office to a hospital bed, to a luxury apartment in the sky, with a guy she had feelings for but wasn't sure what he felt for her—if anything. Being stretched like a rubber band from one emotion to the next was exhausting.

Sylvia was about to remove Dale's hand from her shoulder when she heard barking. She looked past the staff to see a brown-and-white dog of dubious lineage running toward them. Dale stepped from behind her wheelchair and put up a hand. "No, Mutt. Stop!"

Remarkably, the dog skidded to a halt directly in front of Sylvia's wheelchair. Mutt seemed to be an adequate name. With his big, black round eyes, pink tongue hanging out of his mouth, and spotted tail thumping on the floor, he looked to be a cross between a terrier, a bulldog, and something else she couldn't quite identify.

Dale's next move almost had her believing she'd

been rolled into the wrong apartment. Mega-wealthy Dale Forester, CEO of one of the largest real estate firms in the country, smiled as the dog jumped up into his arms and licked his face from ear to ear.

"There's a good dog. I love you, too."

Where was her phone? Dale Forester was cooing. Randi needed to see this, and the urge to snap a video of this love fest and text it to her had Sylvia's fingers itching. The besotted look on Dale's face made her pinch her thigh to keep from laughing out loud.

"Sylvia, meet Mutt."

Mutt barked.

A tall, lean man rushed into the foyer, huffing so hard he looked as if he'd just run a race. "Sorry, Mr. Forester. He heard your voice, and I couldn't stop him. I was just finishing his pedicure."

"It's okay, Justin," Dale said.

The man referred to as Justin wore beige khakis and a yellow polo shirt featuring an embroidered image of a spaniel. The words *UNLEASHED SPA* were displayed prominently across his broad chest.

Inwardly, Sylvia shook her head. Of course, Mutt was cared for by a spa specializing in in-home visits. What else does a man with billions do with his money? What did give her pause was the silly grin on Dale's face as he cuddled his dog. This was a side of him she hadn't expected to see. She raised her eyebrows in mild astonishment.

"Mutt, Sylvia will be staying with us while she gets better." Dale held on to the dog and knelt in front of Sylvia's chair. "Say hello."

Mutt barked twice.

Sylvia couldn't help but smile. If it weren't for the

fact she lived in a shoebox masquerading as an apartment, she most certainly would have had a dog of her own. "Well, hello there, Mutt." She held out her hand for him to sniff. He licked her fingers and then gave two more quick barks. She scratched him behind the ear. "I think we're going to be good friends."

Dale stood, handing the dog over to the groomer, Justin. "Can you give him a walk around the block while we get settled?"

"Sure thing, Mr. Forester."

Leash in hand, Justin carried Mutt toward the elevator.

"Mrs. Traylor, I'll take Sylvia to her room and be back shortly to discuss dinner arrangements."

"Yes, Mr. Forester."

Sylvia took in a deep breath. She'd only been there for ten minutes, and already she could tell this 'Yes, Mr. Forester' stuff would get old fast.

Chapter 20

The staff dispersed to attend to their various duties, leaving Sylvia and Dale alone in the foyer. Wanting to fill the silence as he pushed her wheelchair farther into the apartment, Sylvia said the first thing that popped into her head. "Mutt's adorable."

"I don't know if I'd call him adorable, but he does have a certain charm."

"Actually, I would have expected to see you with a different kind of dog. You know, dogs say a lot about their owners." The wheelchair stopped, and she turned and looked up at Dale—one eyebrow arched.

He bent toward Sylvia and spoke softly into her ear. "Oh, do they? What kind of dog did you have me pegged for?"

The nearness of his lips made her slightly lightheaded. Gripping the arms of the wheelchair, she steeled herself to keep her mind on the topic at hand. "Ahh, I…I don't know." But her response wasn't true. She'd expected him to have an expensive purebred—a shepherd, or even a mastiff. In her mind, his financial status practically demanded it.

"You know, Mutt's special," Dale said. "I found him last spring on one of my runs in the park. I heard whimpering coming from the bushes. I stopped, and with no small amount of wariness, I might add, followed the sound. There was Mutt, injured, scared, and looking half-starved to death. Well, I just couldn't leave him there. So, I took him home, found a vet to tend to his injuries, and, well, we've been friends ever since."

"That was lucky for him," Sylvia said.

"For both of us, really. He's pretty special." Dale cleared his throat. "So, you ready for the grand tour?"

While Sylvia was nearly worn out from all the exertion and could have used a nap, she was enjoying her time with Dale too much to take a break. So, instead of telling him the truth, she looked up and smiled. "Sure, let's go."

He wheeled her down the hall and into an enormous living room, featuring an expanse of floor-to-ceiling windows along its southern wall. The view was breathtaking, encompassing Central Park and stretching to the tip of lower Manhattan and out into New York Harbor.

The room held sleek, modern furniture with low lines which didn't compete with the views. Its muted beige tones were accented by crystal and gold and dotted with angular lamps and light fixtures. Though the look was in direct opposition to her shabby-chic taste, its subtle hues had a calming effect.

Dale wheeled her to the windows, and through the spotless glass, she could feel the warmth of the sun on her face. Her entire body relaxed.

"I love it, too," Dale said.

Sylvia looked up to find him staring. "So, what floor did you say we were on again?"

"I didn't. But we're on fifty. It's a remarkable view, and one of the reasons I bought the apartment."

Sylvia turned toward him. "What's the other

reason?"

"It's big. And I have two floors. Downstairs are my home office and several guest rooms."

She looked back to the one-hundred-and-eighty-degree panorama of Manhattan and the boroughs beyond. She'd never seen anything like it. *This is how the other half lives.* Then she mentally amended the thought—*this is how half-of-the-half-of-the-half of the other half lives*. "Exactly how many rooms are there?"

Dale's eyes shifted up. "Oh, let's see…"

Sylvia watched him; he was obviously counting in his head. The only people who didn't know how many rooms they had were folks with too many.

"There are fifteen–oh, wait, sixteen if you count the laundry area." He held up his hands in a surrender-like motion. "Don't give me that look. Laundry must be done somewhere. Besides, Mrs. Traylor likes it—says she can watch television while she's ironing."

Every inch of the place screamed wealth, and Sylvia had difficulty believing only one person lived in the apartment.

"I can show you where everything is, and of course, you're free to explore if you're up to it." Dale gave a warm smile.

"I really appreciate all you're doing for me, but maybe we could do the rest of the tour another time? I'm pretty drained, and my ankle is beginning to throb. I think I might like to lie down for a while." Sylvia focused on her neatly folded hands in her lap.

"Of course. How stupid of me. You must be exhausted. We'll do this later." He stepped behind her and took hold of the wheelchair. "Your room is just down here." When they reached the end of the long hallway, Dale opened the door and pushed the chair inside. “So, this will be home for as long as you need it.” He stepped in front of the wheelchair and gave a slight bow. “I hope it meets your approval.”

The enormous bedroom faced west, with a spectacular view of the Metropolitan Museum of Art in the distance. Sylvia took a few moments to survey the scene. Mahogany floors gleamed. In one corner, a flower-filled vase stood on a contemporary white dresser. The king-sized bed featured a simple, yet elegant, white duvet with gray-blue piping, the kind she’d only ever seen in magazines. The corners of her mouth lifted, and her inner self did a little happy dance. The room was bigger than her apartment. “This is perfect. I’m sure I’ll be more than comfortable. Thank you.”

“Great. Now, what can I get you? Water? Tea? Or something to eat? You must be starving.”

Sylvia held up a hand. “Please. You’ve done enough, really.”

“But that’s not the point.” He shook his head. “I’m here to help.”

“And you have, Dale. You really have. The truth is, I’m tired. I’d love to take a nap, and that bed looks very inviting.”

“Here, let me help you.” Dale bent toward her.

Sylvia leaned back and raised both hands. “You don’t need to pick me up. I agreed to stay in this wheelchair until we got into the apartment. But now I need to start using the crutches.” She scanned the room. “Do you know where they are?”

“I’ll get them. But maybe you should wait until tomorrow before you start hopping around.”

"Don't worry. I'll follow the doctor's instructions. But let's remember, the only reason I'm in this wheelchair is because you insisted. And while I appreciate all the kindness, I really don't have time to be on the injured list. The sooner I get better, the sooner I can be out of your hair. I don't want to be a burden."

Dale tilted his head and furrowed his brow. "You are *not* a burden. I've got people here who can take care of all your needs."

His last words took her by surprise. Of course, what had she been thinking? He had a staff she could be farmed out to, just like he paid someone to groom and walk his dog. Sylvia turned her head and looked out the window. He played a good game of being concerned, but the only reason she was here was to assuage his guilt for being injured on a Forester property.

"I'll make sure they bring in your crutches. Your suitcase is in the corner, and I'll send Mrs. Traylor in to unpack."

"It's not necessary. I can do it." Sylvia's voice was flat.

"No one doubts your capability to unpack. I just think you should take it easy. It was only yesterday you fell five feet onto your head," Dale said. "Please, I know it's hard, but just try and give your body the rest it needs."

Taking it easy was not something Sylvia Ramirez knew how to do. And now was not the time to rest. She needed to recover quickly and get back to her apartment. She glanced at Dale. How was it possible one moment she had a hundred hummingbirds fluttering inside her every time he looked at her? And the next minute, she wanted to throw darts at his chest.

With an inward sigh, she decided not to try and figure him out. At this moment, the only thing she felt certain of was he didn't feel the same way she did. Sylvia closed her eyes. The thought deflated her, as if someone had plucked a piece of happiness from her soul. "I'd really like to get into something comfortable and sleep a while." The finality in her voice ended any further discussion.

Dale ran his hand through his hair. "If you're sure—but if you need anything, press that button." He pointed to a doorbell ringer mounted along the edge of the end table next to the bed.

"If I do, what happens?"

"It rings in Mrs. Traylor's office off the kitchen, and you can speak through the intercom and tell her what you need."

"Convenient, thanks." Her tone was flippant, but Dale didn't seem to notice. She made a mental note to add this to the list of things she would tell Randi because, of course, everyone had a bell that rang through to their housekeeper.

"Well, then, I'll let you rest. I think we'll eat an early dinner, say six thirty. Is that okay with you?"

Sylvia nodded, and Dale turned and closed the door.

****

Dale had never met anyone more stubborn than Sylvia Ramirez. He'd been surprised when she accepted his offer to stay at his apartment. Despite her standoffish attitude, he smiled as he walked back down the hall. Having her here made him happy.

His phone buzzed, and he retrieved it from his front pocket. The name on the screen belonged to

Leonard Goff, Forester Industries' head of security. He put the phone to his ear. "Leonard, what can you tell me?" Dale's tone was not unfriendly, but it was slightly clipped, and all business.

"Mr. Forester, we now know how the perps got into the construction office site. It would appear one or more intruders used wire cutters to make a small opening in the back fence and crawled through. It must have been right around the time the guards were changing shifts."

"And what time was that?"

"Approximately ten thirty last night."

Dale lowered his voice. "Why wouldn't one of the guards have seen anyone? Moving the stairs away from the trailer should have caught their attention."

"I agree. But one of the regular guards called in sick. They sent in a temp, and at the time of the intrusion, he was in the booth out front, going over the routine with the other guard. They tell me it took about fifteen minutes, and that must have been when the stairs were moved."

The situation seemed surreal, and Dale didn't respond. Nothing like this had ever happened on a Forester site. He leaned against the wall, rubbing his forehead with the palm of his hand.

"Mr. Forester, you there?"

"Yes. I'm here. So, what about the police report?"

"It's been filed with the precinct, but they've found no further evidence. It rained pretty hard in the early hours of the morning, and any footprints left by the perps are long gone. Not to mention it's a construction management site, so there would have been hundreds of prints everywhere."

Dale blew out a breath. "I'm going to need to see a new security plan by tomorrow morning. In the meantime, double the guards."

"Got it."

"We'll talk again in the morning." Dale swiped off his phone and slipped it back into his pocket. The smile on his face and the spring in his step were now replaced by a furrowed brow and hunched shoulders. *This was no accident.*

"Oh, there you are, Mr. Forester."

Dale looked up. Mrs. Traylor was coming toward him.

"Is everything all right, sir?"

"Yes. Fine." Dale forced a smile. "So, what deliciousness will Gretchen be preparing tonight?"

"Well, sir, there are several options."

As the housekeeper recited the various possibilities, Dale only half-listened. His attention was stuck on Sylvia's accident. Whoever moved the steps had to know she would be working late. No matter how many times he'd turned it over in his mind, he couldn't work out who would want to harm her, or why. She was one of the most beloved people in the neighborhood. Whether she liked it or not, he was determined to keep her here until he could discover who was responsible.

Chapter 21

Sylvia plopped down on the edge of the bed in defeat. Her reflection in the full-length mirror on the opposite wall mocked her. For three days, she'd struggled to adapt to the ankle boot and crutches, but her body coordination was all off, and she just couldn't get the hang of it. *Come on, girl, you can do this.*

Blowing a loose strand of hair off her face, she bit down on her lower lip and raised herself off the bed. She tried rolling her shoulders back to ease the tension, but the effort had the opposite effect, producing a trickle of sweat down her back. Gripping the handles of the crutches, she forced herself to stay upright. *This is not the hardest thing you've ever done.*

But the crutches dug deeper into her armpits, and she wanted nothing more than to just lie back on the bed and forget being mobile for the next three weeks. The idea of Dale's staff continuing to wait on her was all the impetus she needed to keep trying. The knock on the door gave her a start.

With a groan, she tilted her head toward the ceiling. She was *so* not in the mood for Mrs. Traylor asking if she needed anything. Everything about her current situation put a crimp in her I-can-take-care-of-myself lifestyle. She exhaled. "Yes?" Impatience rang in her tone.

"It's me, Dale. Can I come in?"

Without waiting for a reply, the door opened.

Sylvia pasted on a half-smile. "Hello." She spoke to Dale's reflection in the mirror. Turning her body to face him required too much energy.

"Hey," Dale said.

"Hey, yourself."

"You okay?"

She waited a beat, debating if she should tell him how she really felt. She decided against it. Vulnerable was not a good look. "I'm fine. Why?"

"You haven't left your room for three days. I can't even get you to come out to join me for dinner. I guess"—he scratched the side of his face—"I was worried."

"Nothing to worry about. I've been a little tired at night, so it's just easier to go to sleep." She worked hard to keep her tone light, but she could feel the tears welling up behind her eyes.

Dale leaned against the door jamb—his eyes downcast.

"What?" His stance unnerved her—putting her on the defensive. "What are you thinking?"

Dale narrowed his gaze. "Are you in pain? Because if you are, I can call the doctor and get you something for the pain."

Sylvia let go of the right crutch and put up a hand, as if to say, no, don't worry. But the momentum of her gesture was unexpected. Before she could get a word out, she felt her body losing its balance. As if in slow motion, she let go of the other crutch, her arms moving in tight circles, waving like a ground crewman guiding an airliner to its gate. "Oh, oh, oh, shooooooot!" She was toppling straight backward.

Dale dove across the bed.

Sylvia came crashing down on top of him.

A stunned silence swept the room as neither moved.

"You okay?" Dale's voice was muffled.

It began as a giggle, but within a millisecond became an uncontrollable laugh. She couldn't help it. The entire scene struck her as hilarious. The thought of Dale squished beneath her turned her giggling into full-throttle laughter.

"Sylvia?"

"Ye-ah?" Sylvia tried to catch her breath. She was laughing so hard her entire body bounced up and down.

"You quishin' ma 'ose."

"Uh-huh." Tears streamed down her face, and her sides ached, but she somehow managed to roll off him and onto her side. She turned to face him and croaked out one word. "Sorry."

Dale lifted his head off the bed and pulled at his nose. "It's all good. It's not broken." He sounded stuffed up.

She leaned her head back and guffawed.

Dale laughed along with her.

When they finally managed to regain their composure, they found themselves facing each other, inches apart. Sylvia thought he was one of the finest-looking men she'd ever been this close to. She wanted to lean in, but Randi's voice suddenly echoed in her head. *Keep your distance.* She rolled over and sat up. "Dale, I'm fine. Don't worry about me."

"From the look of things, I'd say you're not all that fine." He pushed himself up and off the bed.

"What are you talking about?"

"Anyone with two eyes can see you're not exactly an expert with those things yet." He pointed to the crutches sprawled on the floor.

"I'm getting the hang of them. And anyway, the doctor said in a week or two, I won't need them." Sylvia put her attention on her nails, as if she were admiring a new manicure. She'd rather look anywhere than at him.

"Did I ever tell you about the time I broke my leg in two places?" Dale asked.

Sylvia shook her head but didn't look up. Staring into his green eyes would only weaken her resolve.

"Well, do you want to hear about it?"

"I'm all ears." But she still avoided his gaze.

"I was in high school, and I went with my family on a winter ski trip to Switzerland."

Of course, Switzerland. Sylvia gave him a sideways glance. *I mean, if you're gonna ski, where else would you go? Man, are we worlds apart.*

"We went with another family. They were best friends of my parents, and they had a daughter, Millicent—and I thought everything about her was perfect. I was constantly trying to impress her. But she was three years older, and she never gave me a second glance. She didn't even give me a first glance, but boy, did I try to get her to notice me."

Sylvia tried to imagine Dale in need of anyone's attention, but she couldn't picture it.

"Anyway, the year we went skiing, I had just turned fifteen. When we arrived at the hotel, Millicent was standing in the lobby. She was beautiful, and immediately, my heart beat ten times faster, my mouth went dry, and my palms were a sweaty mess. I had it bad. I wanted to say hello, but I didn't trust my voice not to stammer. While I was working out what I could possibly say, a tall, polished guy walked up and kissed her on the mouth." Dale paused. "The whole scene was cringe inducing, and it knocked the wind out of me. A boyfriend? It was a shock."

Why was he telling her this story? Sylvia didn't get it. Although, she had to admit, his vulnerability was fairly appealing.

"Until that moment, I'd never experienced jealousy, and it ate me up. Instead of recognizing I wasn't old enough, and she already had a boyfriend, I stupidly spent the next five days trying to get her to notice me."

"How?" She found Dale's willingness to be so open rather alluring. First rescuing Mutt, and now this. He was turning out to be full of surprises.

He leaned against the dresser. "Well, I won't bore you with every single stupid move—"

"Oh, please, bore me."

Dale crossed his legs. "Are you making fun of me, Ms. Ramirez?"

"Who me?" Sylvia put her hand to her chest.

"I see you smirking. But I'm going to finish this story anyway because I have a point to make."

"I can hardly wait." She widened her eyes in doe-eyed innocence.

"All right. All right. I'll jump to the good part. On the fifth day, I took one of slopes at a greater speed than I normally would have or should have. And it was very steep."

"You mean you were showing off?"

He shook his head. "I mean, I was reckless."

Sylvia tilted her head and narrowed her gaze.

"Oh, all right, I was showing off, too."

"And? What happened?"

"The short version?" Dale scoffed. "I fell off the side of my skis and tumbled down the slope for about two hundred feet, slamming into a bank of trees."

"Ouch, that must have hurt."

Dale briefly closed his eyes and gave a shiver. "Double fracture. They had to airlift me off the mountain. Make no mistake, the physical pain was intense, but my pride sustained the worst of the injuries."

Sylvia laughed. "So, what's your point, Mr. Forester?"

"My point is, I know how it feels to break a bone, and I also know how to walk on crutches without falling on my face. And I can teach you, so you don't stay locked up in this room for the next two weeks."

With a loud exhale, Sylvia straightened. "And what's wrong with staying locked up in here?"

He raised an eyebrow. "Seriously? You really want an answer?"

"I just don't want to be any trouble."

Dale put up a hand. "You're no trouble. Anyway, how would anyone know? You've barely eaten, and you never come out of your room."

"Okay. Okay." She glared. "I hate these stupid crutches. My armpits hurt, and every time I try and take a step, I feel like my nose is going to get up close and personal with the floor."

Dale laughed.

Her eyes widened. "Are you laughing at me?"

"I'm laughing with you."

"But I don't think this is funny."

"Sorry. I'll stop." He put a hand over his mouth

"Thanks." Sylvia gave him half an eye roll.

"Come on. This is easy." Dale clapped his hands. "Seriously, you'll be a champ in no time." He picked up the fallen crutches and handed them to Sylvia. "Come on, take them."

Sylvia huffed.

"Come on." He placed them into her hands. "Now, hold on to them and use them as leverage to raise yourself to a standing position."

"Easy for you to say." Sylvia smirked.

"I'll be right here to catch you if you fall."

"Okay." With the crutches out in front, she pressed down hard and, using her core, lifted herself off the bed. Miraculously, she didn't fall forward and gave a silent thank you for her bi-weekly Pilates. "Now what?" She didn't sound eager.

"I'd say maybe lighten up on the attitude." He grinned.

This time, Sylvia did a full eye roll and a simultaneous head shake.

"Oh, you can do better than that," Dale said.

Sylvia pasted a huge smile on her face. "Better?"

"There you go. Sometimes you have to pretend to enjoy a task, and pretty soon, you'll feel as if you really are enjoying it."

She looked at him from underneath her lashes. "Did you read that off a milk carton?"

This time it was Dale who gave Sylvia an eye roll.

"Okay, okay. Sorry. I'll try."

"Great. So now, you want to place the crutches about a foot out in front. Then lift and swing your body forward and place your good foot where the crutches are." Dale performed a poor imitation of what he wanted her to do. "Simple."

Sylvia gave him a sideways glance.

"Go on. You can do it."

Taking in a breath, she placed the tips of the crutches out in front, a few inches too far from her body. She lurched forward. In an instant, Dale's arms were wrapped around her waist, pulling her close and preventing her nose from getting intimate with the polished mahogany at her feet.

"Whoa, that was close." Dale held on.

The room seemed to spin. The woodsy scent of his cologne and the feel of his arms wrapped around her gave her a dizzying sensation. She tightened her grip on the rubber handles of her crutches and squeezed her eyes shut. *Stop it, girl.*

"You *can* do this." Dale released her. "You just put the crutches out too far. Don't take such a big step. Try it again."

Sylvia took in a breath and squared her shoulders. "Okay."

For the next forty-five minutes, she forced herself to focus on Dale's instructions and not on his touch, or the way his lips curled up to one side when he smiled. When she finally managed to walk ten feet without swaying in any direction, she let out a sigh of relief.

Dale clapped his hands in approval. "I think you're getting the hang of it."

Proficiency with crutches wasn't a life skill she'd ever thought she would need to perfect. But she had to admit, being able to maneuver with greater ease lifted her mood.

"I think you should take your new ability out for a spin," Dale said.

Sylvia shook her head. "I'm not ready to go out. Not yet."

"I meant around the apartment." Dale opened the bedroom door. "Come on. Let's take a look at the view from another angle. You must be bored, stuck in here for the last few days."

Sylvia nodded and headed gingerly for the door. As she started down the hall, she heard clicking sounds and instantly knew it had to be Mutt scurrying across the wooden floor. She stopped, planted her crutches firmly, and held on tight. As she suspected, the dog came skidding around the corner, barking, and running straight for her. Sylvia closed her eyes and braced for impact.

"Mutt! Stop!" Dale demanded.

Sylvia opened one eye and found Mutt sitting inches in front of her, tail wagging, head tilted. "Well, aren't you adorable?" She leaned forward. His chocolate eyes begged her to pick him up.

"He's adorable all right, but you're far from ready to have him jump all over your boot. Tell you what"—Dale picked up his pal—"let's go in the living room and take in the vista. Mutt can sit next to you on the couch."

They made their way down the long hallway toward the sunlight.

Having been cooped up in one of the guest bedrooms for the past three days, Sylvia had almost forgotten this was not like any apartment she'd ever been in. She stopped as they entered the enormous living room and looked out the windows. From up here, it seemed as if they were living in a cloud; it was magical. "You were right."

"About what?" Dale asked.

"This view. It's stunning. Do you ever get tired of it?"

Dale put his hand in his pockets and took a moment before answering. "No. Not tired. But sometimes, I do take it for granted. That's when I know I'm working too much and need to stop and re-examine what it's all for. I wait for the sun to set, shut off all the lights, and just stare out there."

Sylvia studied his face as he looked out upon the city. "You just stare?"

Dale shrugged. "There's a lot that goes on when I stare."

"Like what?"

"Oh, I don't know. Reflection. Decisions. Solutions. And then, finally, quiet."

"I'm not sure I get it."

"Well, I look out at the vastness of the city, and at first, my mind races over a million different things. You know, work, my family, a project that isn't going well, a project that *is* going well. And if I stand here long enough, and look out there long enough, eventually my mind gets quiet. I stop thinking about myself and start thinking about the people down there on the street. The thousands of people with their *own* stories, or situations, or heartaches, or troubles. That's when I realize I have no problems. And that's when my mind seems to shut off. The noise in my head stops. And it's in those moments of clarity I find answers to whatever's bothering me."

Sylvia gave a slow smile. "So that's how your mind works."

"Not all the time, but invariably, after one of my reflective evenings, the next day, I do something right." Dale grinned.

"Right?"

"Yeah." Dale nodded. "Like making the decision to change the Washington Heights project to a proposal that…well…that will benefit more than just the few."

Sylvia looked down at the street below. It all seemed so tiny and far away—the people, the traffic. *So, this is where he comes to solve problems.* He continually surprised her. "I think I'll sit." Her armpits were aching from the crutches. After settling on the sofa, with Mutt across her lap, a wave of exhaustion came over her, and her eyelids became heavy. She stroked Mutt and tried to lean back, but the couch's backrest was too low for her to do anything but sit straight.

"Are you okay? You don't look comfortable," Dale said.

"I don't mean to be ungrateful, but this furniture, beautiful as it is, was not exactly designed with comfort in mind."

Dale scratched the back of his head. "You're right. But I can't take the credit, or the blame. I didn't pick it out."

"Who did? Your decorator?"

"No. My ex."

It surprised Sylvia to hear he had an ex. From all she'd read, Dale was touted as the rich, spoiled playboy. In other words, no attachments. Whatever. It didn't matter because it wasn't any of her business. She was just a guest—an employee. In fact, she was just someone he needed to take care of for a while.

The thought was a reminder to keep Dale at a distance. Otherwise, the small ache in her heart would only grow. "I think I need to head back to the room and lie down. I'm drained after the workout on the crutches."

Dale nodded. His smile slightly fading. "Your body's still healing, so take as much rest as you need." He held out his hand. "Come on, Mutt. Let's get Sylvia back to her room."

The next morning, she woke to a text from Dale. He'd flown to the Buffalo worksite again. She stretched her arms overhead. "Why didn't he tell me yesterday?" She stared up at the ceiling. "Sheesh." Dale needed to be exorcised from her mind. Or better yet—get this boot off her foot and get as far away from him as possible.

Chapter 22

For the first time in forever, Sylvia felt lonely. Randi was in Puerto Rico, Dale was out of town, and the community center was closed. The only cure she knew for loneliness was food and lots of it. Since she'd become more proficient on the crutches, it seemed as good a time as any to try out her newfound independence. She hobbled her way out of her room toward sustenance and people.

The kitchen didn't face the park, but they were up high enough that sunlight flooded in through a wall of windows over the sink, inviting her in. "Good morning, Gretchen."

Gretchen raised her eyebrows. "Good morning, Ms. Ramirez."

"Please, call me Sylvia." She smiled and headed for the refrigerator.

"Is there something I can get you?"

Gretchen's chilly reception nearly convinced Sylvia to take an apple from the fruit bowl on the marble countertop and leave, without handling her craving for bacon and eggs. "I'm good. Thanks." She peered into the largest custom cooler she'd ever seen.

Gretchen moved close, pulling out the egg carton. "How do you like them cooked?"

Sylvia straightened and leaned on her crutches. "I really don't want to put you through any trouble." And the truth was, she didn't. But as she gripped the handles of her crutches, she realized it would take a herculean effort on her part to maneuver around the large kitchen to prep and cook her breakfast, all while hopping on one foot. She sighed. "Scrambled hard, if you don't mind."

"Anything else?" Gretchen asked. This time, her smile seemed genuine.

"Really, don't go to anymore—"

"Ms. Ramirez…sorry, Sylvia." She shook her head. "I'm a chef for a reason. I love to cook. It's what I do. Please tell me what you desire for breakfast, and I'll be more than happy to prepare it."

When Gretchen dropped the formality and called her by her first name, the anxiety Sylvia had been holding in her chest evaporated. "You know what an-all-you-can-eat breakfast is?"

With an open-mouthed grin, Gretchen set about pulling out bowls from custom cabinets and buttering pans on the twelve-burner range. "One all-you-can-eat coming up."

When she heard a bark, Sylvia turned to find Mutt scampering into the kitchen, followed by Mrs. Traylor.

The housekeeper stopped just inside the doorway. "Oh. Good morning, Ms. Ramirez."

"Hi." Sylvia bent to pet Mutt, who was wagging his tail like a metronome set at *prestissimo*.

"I'll just get a cup of coffee and be out of your way," Mrs. Traylor said.

"Please, don't let me interrupt your morning routine." Sylvia motioned for Mrs. Traylor to join her at the table. "Sit down. I'm sorry if I've invaded your space. It's just that I'm tired of eating alone, and this room is so inviting. When I was growing up, the kitchen was the gathering place for all occasions."

"In my home, too," Gretchen said.

Mrs. Traylor seemed to visibly relax. She headed for the copper cappuccino maker and began spooning espresso into the portafilter. "It was the same for me." She offered a conservative smile.

"If you haven't had breakfast yet, Gretchen's rustling up an all-you-can-eat."

Mrs. Traylor's eyes lit up. "Oh, goody, it's been ages since I stuffed myself. Eggs, bacon, cheese, and toast. How sinful." She giggled.

The three of them spent the next hour eating, gabbing, and laughing. With each passing minute, Sylvia felt more relaxed. She hadn't realized how much she missed conversation. What she hadn't expected was learning new things about Dale. It wasn't as if she'd brought up the subject; both women seemed all too willing to discuss their employer, and she was all too happy to listen.

Apparently, Sylvia had been the first woman to live in the apartment. Even his last serious girlfriend, his ex as he'd called her, the one with a taste in uncomfortable furniture, hadn't actually lived in the penthouse.

"I've never seen Mr. Forrester so attentive. For the last three days, he's called practically every hour to check on how you were doing," Mrs. Traylor commented.

Gretchen nodded. "He checked the menu with me twice each day. He's never done that before."

Sylvia smiled. She knew it was unwise to care what Dale Forester thought, but her mind—no, make that her heart—still wasn't getting the message.

For the rest of the week, while Dale was at the construction site in Buffalo, Sylvia immersed herself in work. Several times each day, she coordinated community center business with Randi via videoconference. Today's call focused on helping several storeowners in the Washington Heights neighborhood secure bank loans, making it easier to lease retail space on the ground floors of the new apartment buildings. When they'd finished discussing the last item on the day's to-do list, Sylvia sat back and took a sip of iced tea. "So, how's the move going with your mom?"

Randi leaned in until her face filled Sylvia's screen. "I forgot how much she loves me." She spoke in a conspiratorial whisper.

Sylvia leaned forward and whispered back, "What do you mean?"

"You know my mother; she shows her love by criticizing everything I do. I forgot how annoying it is."

"Oh, come on. You were dying to see her. It can't be that bad already. You haven't been there long."

Randi looked over her shoulder and continued to whisper, "Trust me. The reunion got old fast. It usually takes a few weeks before she starts in with the nitpicking. Maybe she's nervous about the move, because she went from zero to sixty on the critical meter in the time it takes to fry a plantain."

"*Ay*, *mi hija*. Too much salt in the beans."

"*Ay*, Randi, how much water did you put in the plants? Are you trying to drown them?"

"*Ay*, what are you wearing, *mi hija*? You're going to church, not a club.'"

"*¡Ay! ¡Ay! ¡Ay!* I want to scream." Randi clenched

her fists at the side of her head and then spread her fingers in an explosion-like motion. "But I can't. She's my mother, and I love her. I'd do anything for her. But man, how quickly she forgets, I'm twenty-four and an actual adult."

Sylvia laughed. "Oh, girl, I don't envy you. Are you almost finished packing up the house?"

Randi nodded. "She's moving into the cutest condo. If I ever wanted to live in San Juan, I'd get an apartment in her building. Right on the beach. Just fabulous."

"Well, now we know where we're going on our next vacation."

"We could only stay here two days, tops, before she started in on the *Ay, mi hijas,* plural."

"Ha! Okay, we'll go someplace else. So, when do you think you'll be home?"

Randi raised her eyebrows. "Why, you miss me?"

"Hell to the yes. I'm all by myself."

"Where's *Señor Guapo*?" Randi put her elbow on the table and rested her chin in a hand. "Still gorgeous, I suppose?"

"He's working in upstate New York this week. Buffalo, I think."

"I thought he was taking care of you?" Randi's voice rose an octave.

Sylvia crossed her arms over her chest. "I don't need him. I've got Gretchen, his chef, and Mrs. Traylor, the housekeeper, and they're terrific."

"Two people waiting on you hand and foot? *¡Que vida!*"

"Oh, *puh-leaze*." Sylvia blew out a long breath. "This is a short-term lifestyle. Remember?"

"Yeah, I know. But I'm glad you've got people taking care of you while I'm not there. It's bad enough you're working so hard."

"Work is the only thing keeping me sane." Sylvia sighed.

Randi pursed her lips. "I still worry about you."

"There's nothing to worry about. I'm fine." Another sigh.

"If everything's fine, what's all the heavy breathing about? That's like the third major exhalation since we got on this call."

"Oh, I don't know." She exhaled once more.

"See, there it is again."

"I guess if I had to give it a name—I'm a little lonely."

"Lonely?"

Sylvia nodded.

"As if." Randi scoffed. "How can that be? We talk at least five times a day. And you just told me you've got two people hovering all over you."

"Gretchen and Mrs. Traylor are nice and really helpful, but they have jobs to do. And they're not my friends. Not like you. And sure, we talk a lot, but you know there's no substitute for in-person human contact."

Randi snorted. "What's this really about? It's not like you to be so down. The last time I saw you this—" She stopped short and snapped her fingers. "Hold up. The last time you carried on like you just lost something you couldn't live without was when Julian ghosted you."

Sylvia sat forward. Her face felt as if it were on fire. *I'm so busted.* But she wasn't going to give Randi the satisfaction. So, she decided to go on the defensive. "Give me a break. That's *so* not true." She rolled her eyes toward the ceiling.

Randi held up a hand. "Don't even. This *is* about Dale, isn't it? I can't believe it. Have you learned nothing? Your heart was in pieces after Julian. I didn't think you'd want to go through that again."

Sylvia tilted her head and frowned. "What are you blah, blah, blahing about?" She made a motion with her hand, imitating a flapping mouth. "Just say it."

"Oh, man. How many times do I need to spell it out?" Randi shook her head and leaned into the camera. "Okay. Dale Forester is wrong for you. Did you really need me to repeat it yet again?"

In her heart, she knew Randi was right. She didn't fit into this life—the expensive furnishings, the staff, the fact that each window in the apartment laid Manhattan at her feet. She needed to get her head out of these penthouse clouds and get better. Because the longer she stayed, the more she wanted to stay. Counting the days until Dale's return had become an exhausting exercise.

"I finished the proposal for the funding for the new computers. I'll email it. Let me know if it needs anything else," Sylvia said.

"Whoa." Randi blinked several times. "You changed the subject so fast I nearly got whiplash."

"Yup. Moving on." Her tone said there would be no more talk of Dale Forester.

Randi shrugged. "If you say so. Moving on."

They discussed the computer proposal, and then Sylvia called it an early night, claiming exhaustion. Instead, she went to her room, lay down, and, despite herself, thought about Dale.

During his stay in Buffalo, she had received dozens of texts and emails from him, all relating to business, but they hadn't spoken by phone in almost a week. Each time hers rang, her heart lifted for a moment, only to deflate again when the caller ID indicated it wasn't him.

By day five, after checking her email and her phone for the twentieth time, she gave herself a mental pep talk. *The most important thing is the center. You cannot care for this guy. Besides, you were lucky this time—only your feelings got bruised. At least you didn't give your heart away.*

She knew the last part wasn't true, because the ache in her chest was real.

Chapter 23

The moment Dale stepped off the elevator, he heard nails clacking against the hardwood floor.

Within seconds, Mutt skidded into the foyer.

"Hi, there!" Dale bent down and let the excited canine lick his face. "Oh, there's a good boy. I'm happy to see you, too."

Mutt barked twice.

Dale scratched him behind the ears. Being home again had the effect of a weight lifting off his chest. He removed his jacket, draped it over his shoulder, and headed toward the wall of windows in the living room. He took in a cleansing breath and looked out onto the streets below.

The last five days had felt like five months. The unexpected business trip had thrown off the rest of his schedule, and he'd been forced to work almost around the clock to keep up. But he'd had no choice. Returning to the Buffalo construction site was imperative. The project had incurred far too many unjustified delays and unexpected costs. He'd thought it would be prudent to show up again, this time unannounced.

On his arrival, he hadn't liked what he'd seen. The work was slow, sloppy, and the books had revealed not only skyrocketing costs, but also payments against expenses which had nothing to do with the project. He had left the site, instructing his comptroller to dig further into the books over the weekend.

"Welcome home, Mr. Forester. We didn't expect you back until the end of next week."

Dale turned to face Mrs. Traylor. "Thanks. I didn't expect to be here either. But there wasn't much more I could accomplish this weekend, so I decided to spend it at home."

"Will you be dining in?"

Dale checked his watch. "Ah. It's almost that time. Yes. I'll be eating in."

"Very good. I'll let Ms. Ramirez know."

Dale's heart skipped a beat. Dinner with Sylvia. A nice way to end what had been a difficult week. "Uh, hold on." He put his finger to his bottom lip. "You know, please don't alert Ms. Ramirez I'm back. I'd rather like to surprise her, if you don't mind. What time is dinner?"

"In about thirty minutes."

"Great, just enough time to wash up."

"Very good, sir."

Dale found his mood lightened, knowing he would be dining with Sylvia. He had hoped being away would have dulled his growing obsession, but he found it had only gotten stronger. And now that he was finally home, he realized he couldn't wait to see her. In fact, the thought sent a small, unfamiliar jolt through him. He was excited and nervous all at once. The feelings were like he was fifteen again, with that mad crush on Millicent. No woman had made him feel like that since, except for Sylvia. Spending the evening with her felt like the exact remedy to take him out of his funk and take his mind off the company's problems. But first, he needed to wash off the past week.

He walked into his ensuite bathroom, turned on the jet spray, and quickly undressed. He found himself hurrying, anxious to stare into her deep brown eyes again. The anxiety made his mouth dry— as if he was going on a first date with a girl he really liked. *Oh, Dale, man! You got it bad. Get. A. Grip.* He chuckled. *I'm even starting to talk like her.*

He finished showering in record time. Within five minutes, he toweled off, brushed his teeth, and ran his fingers through his hair. Checking himself in the mirror, he saw a slight dark stubble, but he didn't want to take the time to shave. He quickly threw on a pair of khakis and a blue button-down shirt.

The dining room lights had been dimmed, and the table was set for two. He walked over to the sideboard and poured himself a glass of twenty-year-old bourbon over ice. He turned when he heard Mutt bark.

"Oh, I didn't think you were home." Sylvia stood in the entranceway. "When did you get here?"

Stunning. That was the word that came to mind. Shiny brown curls fell over her shoulders. Her face seemed to glow, with her cheeks slightly flushed. He rested his eyes for a moment on her full lips, then on the gauzy material of her sleeveless, muted-green dress; it seemed nearly transparent. He was speechless.

"*Helloooo?*" Sylvia asked. "Is something wrong?"

Dale straightened and closed his mouth. "Hi." He lifted his glass in her direction. "Wow, look at you. Off the crutches." He had no idea why those were the first words out of his mouth. *Yes, you do. She makes you nervous*. What he'd wanted to say was that she was beautiful. He'd missed her. He hadn't realized how much until just now.

Sylvia looked down at her booted foot. “Yes, and I think this thing comes off next week, so it looks like I’ll soon be out of your way.”

The idea of Sylvia leaving produced a visceral reaction, as if he could feel an actual physical loss. He chose to ignore her comment. “How’s the pain?”

“I hardly notice it anymore.”

“Wonderful. Um, would you care for a drink?” He pointed to the decanter on the sideboard.

Sylvia shook her head. “Not just yet. I’ll have wine with dinner.”

Dale was afraid to lift the glass to his lips for fear he’d reveal his shaking hand. *You need to grab hold of yourself and stop acting like this is the first time you’ve ever had dinner with a woman.*

“Shall we?”

Dale blinked and realized Sylvia had asked him a question. “Huh?”

“Shall we? Sit, I mean,” Sylvia repeated.

“Oh, of course. Here, let me get your chair.” Dale put his glass on the table and hurried to her side.

But Sylvia put up her hand. “Not necessary. But thanks. I’ve gotten quite proficient at all things.”

“All things, you say?” Dale pulled her chair out over her objections, and then seated himself across from her, putting a linen napkin in his lap.

“Well, I have to admit the boot makes it a bit difficult to take a bath.”

“Yeah, I remember when I broke my leg and having to rest it on the side of the tub so the cast wouldn’t get wet. But getting down *into* the tub on only one leg, while keeping the other one out of the water, now that was tricky.”

Sylvia laughed.

Dale smiled. The sound of her laugh released a feeling of happiness within him. As if someone had thrown open a window and wind chimes streamed in on a waft of fresh air.

"You're right about that. I was telling Randi I was thankful for all the Pilates classes I've taken. All the lowering and lifting to get in and out of the tub has put my core to the test."

Gretchen stepped into the dining room. "Excuse me, Mr. Forester. Are you ready for dinner?"

Dale nodded.

"Excuse me, Mr. Forester." This time, Marc, one of his assistants, stopped at the far entrance to the dining room. "Oh, sorry, didn't realize you weren't alone."

"It's fine, Marc. What do you need?"

"It's these papers. They need your signature tonight."

Dale beckoned him with his hand. "Sure. Bring them over."

As he approached the dining table, Marc's cell rang, and he answered it. "It's for you, Mr. Forester." He handed his phone to Dale. "It's Leonard Goff."

Dale turned to Sylvia. "Excuse me. I need to take this."

Dale and his assistant moved out of the dining room. Once they were in the hallway, he held Marc's phone to his ear. "Do you have a suspect?" he asked his head of security.

"Mr. Forester," the voice said, "we were able to get a match from the on-site security cameras against police photos. They brought the guy in for questioning. Looks like he was paid to do the job, but he doesn't know by whom."

"How is that possible?" Dale started to pace.

"We're looking into it, and we think we might have a lead."

"Who?"

"We're not there yet, sir. I'll have more information on Monday. Please, sir, be patient."

Dale gritted his teeth. "I don't pay you to tell me to be pat—" He stopped himself. The idea that someone had intentionally hurt Sylvia was unthinkable. "Sorry, Leonard. I'm anxious to get to the bottom of this."

"I understand, sir, and we'll get you answers as quickly as possible."

Dale swiped the phone off and handed it back to his assistant. "Thanks, Marc. This stays between us."

Marc nodded. "Of course."

"I'll sign those now." Dale nodded to the papers in Marc's hand. "It's been one hell of a week, and next week looks just as jam-packed." He signed the papers with a flourish and handed them back. "So, I think it's time for you to take off. Have a nice weekend and recharge."

"Thanks, Mr. Forester. You, too."

Dale took in a deep breath, placed a smile on his face, and walked back into the dining room. "Sorry. I had to take the call. But we won't be disturbed again."

"I understand," Sylvia said. "Sometimes work doesn't know what time it is."

Gretchen opened the door from the kitchen. "Mr. Forester, are you ready?"

Dale nodded.

Gretchen entered with an arugula salad, placed it on the table, and began to serve.

As much as he liked and appreciated his staff, he'd never realized how much they were involved in his life. While he was home, he was never alone.

Chapter 24

Sylvia opened her eyes and glanced at the clock on the side table. The digital numbers read 7:05. She yawned, raised her hands toward the ceiling, and executed a long stretch. Curling onto her side, she closed her eyes again and smiled, her mind presenting her with images of the night before. They'd stayed up well past midnight, playing chess. Years had passed since she played, and she'd forgotten how much she enjoyed the intellectual challenge.

As the evening progressed, she and Dale had become more relaxed and fell into the way they'd been before her accident; enjoying each other's company, easy conversation, and more than a little flirting.

She let out a long sigh and forced her mind into the present, reminding herself women like her didn't have lasting relationships with guys like Dale Forester.

The knock on the door stopped her mind from playing the inevitable twenty rounds of should I-like-him-or-should-I-just-cut-my-losses-right-now?

"Sylvia, you awake? Are you hungry?"

She sat upright like a shot and quickly pulled the covers up to her chin. She hadn't expected to hear Dale's voice.

"Breakfast will be ready in five," he called.

"Okay." The word came out like a croak. She sank back into the covers, listening to his retreating footsteps. *What is Dale doing waking me up? And where is Mrs. Traylor?*

Curiosity finally getting the better of her, she got out of bed and hustled to wash up and throw on sweats. Twenty minutes later, she arrived in the dining room, only to find it empty. "Hello. Anybody here? Mrs. Traylor?"

"In here," Dale said.

Sylvia followed his voice into the kitchen.

"Good morning." Dale's greeting was sing-songy and full of cheer.

Sylvia stopped dead in the doorway, mouth open, shocked to find him standing at the twelve-burner stove with an array of pots and pans, dressed in jeans and a T-shirt, his feet bare. *Dang, those jeans are a nice fit.* Her mouth went dry, and she had to remind herself that this—all of this—would soon be over, and the reality of her five-floor walkup studio apartment would soon hit her like a door that only swings one way. She cleared her throat. "What are you doing?"

Dale turned, his green eyes smiling. "What does it look like?"

"But why? Where are Gretchen and Mrs. Traylor?"

"I gave them the weekend off."

Noting his casual tone, she tried not to make a big deal about it. "Really? Why?"

"They've been working round the clock. They deserved it." Dale shrugged and cracked several eggs into a large bowl. "I had to promise I'd be at your beck and call."

"Uh, that's really not necessary." She hoped the heat creeping up her face wasn't showing.

"I'm making you my famous coconut French toast,

with strawberries and maple syrup."

The heavenly smell of cinnamon and vanilla filled the air, making her stomach grumble. "Smells delicious." Inching her way onto a stool at the chef's island, she watched Dale expertly maneuver about the kitchen. As he whisked the ingredients together, his biceps flexed, and a lock of hair fell over his forehead. Randi was right, she thought. *Señor Guapo*. One fine specimen.

"What are you smiling about?" Dale asked.

Realizing she'd been sitting there sporting a wide grin, she quickly relaxed her face. "Um, nothing. I was just…mentally counting the calories and wondering if I should have two or three pieces." While it made for a plausible answer, it definitely wasn't what she'd been thinking.

Dale plated their breakfast and sat. "*Buen provecho*," he said.

"Ah, you remembered. *Buen provecho*." Sylvia lifted the small glass pitcher in a salute gesture, poured maple syrup over her French toast, cut off a piece, and took a bite. Her mouth filled with sweetness. "Mmmmmmm! Man, that is the *bomb*."

Dale smiled. "Glad you like it."

The next twenty minutes passed in comfortable silence while they ate.

"More coffee?" Dale asked.

"No, thanks." Sylvia pushed her plate away. "But thanks for breakfast. It was scrumptious. I'd never think to make French toast with coconut, and I admit I was skeptical. But now I'm a convert. The combo definitely works. If you ever change your mind about careers, you could take up cooking."

Dale's eyebrows rose over the rim of his coffee cup.

"Seriously, I mean it. Actually, I think you could probably be a TV chef. I mean, damn, you're hot enough. You'd get ratings because women would want to see you at the stove." *Oh, man, did I just say that out loud?* She squeezed her eyes shut. Warmth spread up her neck and across her face. She was certain her cheeks were the color of a Red Delicious apple. "Shoot, I didn't mean that. For a minute, I thought I was talking to Randi."

"Do I look like Randi?"

"No, it's just…well…you make me feel comfortable. I forgot where I was for a second."

Dale laughed. "I accept the compliment, but I'm not changing careers anytime soon. What you just ate is the only thing I know how to cook."

The heat in her cheeks hadn't abated, and neither had the feeling of mortification lodged in the pit of her stomach. "Okay, well, then, thank you for a lovely meal. If you'll excuse me, I'm going to change out of my sweats." She stood and pushed the stool under the counter.

Still laughing, Dale reached out and put his hand on her forearm. "Wait. Stop, Sylvia. Don't go."

"I'm so embarrassed…let me just apologize and make a graceful exit."

"Listen, it's forgotten."

But Sylvia persisted, feeling the need to explain. "I am so sorry—"

"Really"—Dale put his finger to her lips—"it's no big thing."

His touch created such a jolt of electricity she was

sure her hair must be standing on end. All movement in the room seemed to stop. He stepped closer and stared into her eyes. Sylvia was powerless to move as he slowly bent toward her. The beating of her heart was like a marching band on steroids, and if he didn't kiss her soon, she was certain she'd pass out. With their lips inches apart, she closed her eyes and waited for him to seal the deal.

Then his phone rang.

At the unexpected sound, Sylvia's eyes flew open.

Dale reached into his jeans pocket and pulled out his mobile, checking the caller ID. "I need to take this. Please don't go. Just wait here."

Asking her to wait had been wholly unnecessary. He owed her a kiss, and that very thought had her cemented to the spot. "Yes, that's correct…great. Thanks for taking care of everything." She heard him say.

Dale swiped off the call.

"Everything okay?" Sylvia asked.

"Perfect." Dale flashed a smile.

"What's going on?"

"Nothing." He raised his arms in a search-me pose.

"That's not nothing. You've got that I've-got-a-secret look on your face."

"Okay, maybe I have."

"Really?" She waited. "What?"

"Well, for one thing, you've been cooped up in this apartment for days. It's time for some fresh air—"

"There's a reason I haven't exactly been mobile." Sylvia pointed to the boot on her foot.

"I'm well aware of your condition, Ms. Ramirez, but I have a plan."

"You do?"

"Yes, I do, but first, I'm gonna clean up in here."

Smacking her forehead with the palm of her hand, she looked around the kitchen. "What was I thinking, just walking out like that? You cooked. I'll clean."

"Oh, no, you don't." Dale shook his head. "I've got this. Besides, Randi would have my head if she found out you lifted a finger. No. You just go get dressed, and I'll meet you in the front hall in one hour. Will that give you enough time?"

Sylvia tilted her head. "Enough time for what?"

"To get ready for an adventure."

Sylvia stared, not moving.

Dale made a shooing motion. "The quicker you get ready, the quicker we can start. And, uh, dress casual."

"I'm going, I'm going. Sheesh, you're pushy." She headed toward the kitchen door. "So, what are we doing?"

"It's a surprise."

"Fine, but what am I supposed to be wearing to this surprise?" Sylvia asked, hoping it would give her a hint as to where they were headed.

"Like I said, it's very casual." Dale picked up the breakfast dishes and put them in the sink.

An adventure? The thought of one-on-one time with Dale had her insides performing a happy dance. As she walked toward her room, she heard a tiny voice in the back of her mind whisper, "What are you doing?" She stopped in her tracks. The voice sounded suspiciously like Randi's.

****

Several minutes before noon, Dale pulled his SUV into the parking lot of the West 79th Street Boat Basin.

He smiled and turned to face Sylvia—excited to finally reveal his surprise. "Here we are."

Sylvia looked out the window. "What are we doing at the Hudson River?"

"You'll find out. Just stay right there."

"But—"

"No buts." He got out, jogged to the passenger's side, and opened Sylvia's door. "Okay, put your arms around my neck."

"What in the world are you doing?" Sylvia said.

"It's faster if I carry you." Dale reached in and lifted her out of her seat.

"Oh, come on. Put me down. I can walk."

"Wel-l-l-l-l, that might be overstating it." He lifted her in his arms. The closeness gave his heart a jolt. He didn't want to let her go. "For sure you've gotten better, but it's more of a hobble than a walk, so it'll be easier if I carry you. We don't have all day." He shut her door with his foot, ending any argument before it started. "See that boat over there?"

"You're changing the subject."

"As a matter of fact, I am. We're now talking about that boat over there." Dale nodded toward the craft in question.

"You mean that, uh…enormous yacht-like thing in the water?" Sylvia's jaw dropped.

"Yes. That one." He couldn't help but grin. "We're going for a trip."

Sylvia started to laugh as he carried her down the length of the dock. "Where are you taking me?"

"I thought you might enjoy an afternoon adventure sailing up the Hudson." He continued toward the sleek, fifty-foot vessel.

"That's yours?" Sylvia's eyes widened.

Dale remained silent.

Sylvia looked from beneath her lashes. "What was I thinking? Of course, it's yours. You would never *rent* a yacht."

"Are you trying to be funny, or do I detect a not-so-subtle dig?"

Putting a hand to her heart, Sylvia batted her eyelashes. "*Moi*, sarcastic? What gave you that idea?"

Sylvia was flirting. Or at least her version of flirting, which included the subtle and not-so-subtle barbs. Dale simply laughed out loud. Nothing could spoil this day for him. A cloudless cobalt sky, a slight breeze in the air, and this beautiful woman in his arms. This was turning out to be a most perfect morning. As he approached the gangway, he heard the throbbing of the yacht's engines.

The captain and two crew members greeted them and helped them aboard.

While Dale had two other yachts—one anchored off the Amalfi coast, the other in St. Tropez—this was his favorite. Her name was *Journey*, and she was the one he preferred when he wanted to sail to the Caribbean or to just spend time away from everything and everybody. Fitted with every amenity, the boat had a full galley, sleeping quarters for ten, a dining room, and a pool on the upper deck.

When he reached the luxurious aft deck, Dale set Sylvia down on one of the curving, buttery-leather modular couches lining the perimeter. He held his breath as he watched her take in her surroundings.

When he'd thought up this little excursion last night, he wasn't sure how she might react. He'd hoped she'd be surprised and impressed. But now, seeing her sitting here in one of his favorite places, with the soft breeze blowing her chestnut hair, a smile on her face and joy in her eyes, he realized his aim had been simply to make her happy.

After several minutes, Sylvia broke the silence. "This is…well, I'm not sure I have words. It's impressive. I'll say that."

"Glad you like it." Dale picked up a phone embedded in a side console and pressed a button. "We're ready to set sail. Thanks."

"Who was that?" Sylvia asked.

"The captain."

Sylvia shook her head. "This is all so surreal. When did you have time to plan it?"

"Oh, I have my ways." In truth, the thought came in the middle of the night. After their final chess game ended and Sylvia had retired to her room, he knew he needed to do something to get more alone-time with her. When they were apart, he felt less alive.

He'd fired off an email to the yacht's First Officer, instructing him to get everything in motion. He'd been giddy with anticipation since. The nervous, anxious, sweaty-palm feeling hadn't left him all morning. Sylvia had a way of making him feel fifteen all over again.

The engines revved, and the yacht began edging away from the dock.

"Hungry? I had the staff prepare us something to eat."

"After our enormous breakfast? How 'bout we sit and watch the scenery for a bit before we eat again. Is that okay?"

Dale nodded and eased down next to her, happy to

do whatever she wanted. "Are you comfortable?"

"I'm great." She smiled. "What are you staring at?"

"You." Caught in her spell, he was helpless to say otherwise.

"Me, when all of Manhattan is gliding by? Don't tell me you've become jaded to the island's charms."

"No. It's just when I look at you, I find all the beauty I need. I could drown in your chocolate eyes." The sound of a yeoman clearing his throat made Dale look up. "Yes?"

"Would you and Ms. Ramirez care for anything to drink?"

"Not yet, thank you. I'll call you when we're ready." Dale waited for the crew member to be out of sight before putting his arm around Sylvia and drawing her closer. He inwardly sighed, his shoulders relaxing. Sitting here with her felt so right. She was different in so many ways, and seemingly overnight, he'd lost his heart.

The majesty of the Manhattan skyline drifted by. Yet, Dale couldn't take his gaze off Sylvia. The smile on her face as she took it all in brought him a sense of joy he had never experienced.

"Look!" Sylvia pointed to her right. "The Cloisters." She stood to walk toward the rail.

After an awkward first step with her ankle boot, Dale picked her up and carried her.

"You really do need to stop hauling me all over the place."

"Why should I?"

"Because I could get used to it."

"That's fine by me." Dale gently put her down.

Sylvia held on to the railing.

Dale stood behind her, wrapping his arms around her waist. She leaned into him and it nearly took his breath away. He could have stayed like this forever—holding on to Sylvia, staring out over the river.

"Oh, Dale, you remembered"— Sylvia turned to face him, her smile wide—"I've always dreamed of sailing up the Hudson, and you made it happen. It's perfect."

Thrilled he'd made her happy, he stared into her eyes. "It sure is."

Over the next few hours, the yacht sailed as far as Bear Mountain, some thirty miles to the north, before turning back. They drank champagne, accompanied by a magnificent fiery sunset reflected against the million windows of the Manhattan skyline. It had been a perfect day in every way.

As the boat was pulling into the dock, his phone chimed with an incoming text. Dale looked at the message and scowled.

"Something wrong?" Sylvia asked.

"No. Nothing." Dale tried to brush it off, but a message from his comptroller asking for a quick meeting couldn't be good. Dale pocketed his phone and forced a smile. He'd deal with it as soon as they got back to the penthouse. This wasn't going to be such a perfect day after all.

****

The alarm played a soothing melody. Sylvia raised herself up on her elbows and squinted at her phone's digital readout. "Whoever's in charge of this universe really needs to put another day between Saturday and Sunday." She pressed Snooze, flopped back onto the bed, and performed a little shimmy under the covers.

The weekend had been magical. Each hour she'd spent with Dale, her feelings grew exponentially. Without a doubt, she was free-falling with no safety net. The sound of the second alarm nudged her out of her reverie. Glowering at her phone, she reached for it and swiped it off. "Okay, okay. I know it's time to start the day. I'm up."

When she finished bathing and dressing, she looked around the room she'd called home for the last three weeks and sighed. She'd been off crutches for several days, and the boot would soon be removed. The time had come to go back to her apartment—to her real life. Besides, Randi had returned from Puerto Rico; if Sylvia needed anything, Randi lived two blocks away.

But last night, when she'd mentioned leaving, Dale had been adamant she stay a while longer, at least until they had more answers as to who had moved the steps and caused her injuries. She'd thought he was being overly protective, but his insistence had her agreeing to stay until the end of the week.

The question weighing on her mind was whether he would still be interested once she moved out.

Her phone rang, pulling her out of her thoughts. When she saw the number on the screen, she smiled and immediately hit Accept. "Hey, Randi. Welcome home! How was the flight?"

"You sound so normal. Even cheery," Randi said.

"Of course, why wouldn't I be?" She nestled the phone between her left ear and shoulder and put an earring into the right.

"Oh, man. Girl, you haven't heard, have you?"

"Heard what?" Sylvia scrunched her forehead.

"Turn on the television," Randi said.

“There isn’t one in this room.”

“You mean to tell me that gazillion-dollar penthouse doesn’t have a flat-screen on every wall?”

“What could be so important it can’t wait?” Sylvia huffed.

“I’ll hold on while you go find one. Forester Industries is all over the news.”

“Again? What happened? Randi, please just tell me what’s going on.” Sylvia closed her eyes, hoping this was Randi being dramatic.

“Look, why don’t you come over to my apartment, and we’ll talk.”

“You’ve got me all nervous. I can’t wait. I’ll call you back.” Sylvia swiped off the call. Opening a web browser on her phone, she typed in *Forester Industries.* Within seconds, dozens of entries appeared. She scrolled the headlines in open-mouth horror as one headline after the next told a story of kickbacks and deceptive practices. Two articles featured Dale’s name prominently in the headline, and she quickly skimmed them. When she was done, she put a hand over her mouth. “This can’t be true.” She shook her head. “This just can’t be true.”

Had he been lying? All this time, she thought he’d been doing the right thing with the Washington Heights development. Was it possible he’d actually been using her as a public relations shield? Showing the world Forester Industries was performing a meaningful service to the community, but all the while making and taking payoffs?

Despite the pain in her foot, anger fueled her as she hustled to the stairway leading to the apartment’s lower floor in search of Dale. She wanted to confront him, hoping he'd tell her this was all a big misunderstanding and he knew nothing about payoffs or bribes. He couldn't be involved. *He just couldn't.*

As she reached to open the door to his study, she heard Dale's angry voice. It sounded like he was on the phone.

"Of course, I had my suspicions something was wrong. That's why I made all those trips to Buffalo….no, listen, that was just the first step. I planned to do more investigation—" He stopped speaking.

Sylvia wished she knew who was on the other end of the line. She put her ear to the door and held her breath until Dale spoke again.

"I didn't tell anyone because I knew we couldn't withstand the publicity if it got out."

Sylvia let go of the doorknob as if it were made of hot lava. Had she heard correctly? Dale knew about the corruption and intended to bury the information? He wasn't man enough to face the problem? Then who was he? She couldn't bear to hear anymore.

With tears streaming down her face, she staggered up the steps and back to her bedroom. Once inside, she leaned against the dresser to stop the room from spinning. Beads of sweat trickled down her back, and nausea nearly made her knees buckle. Sylvia closed her eyes and took long deep breaths. When she thought she could hold the bile down, she threw her laptop and a few personal items into her shoulder bag. She had to get away before he got off the phone. She didn't want to talk to him. What was there to talk about? Just as she had initially suspected, rich people thought they could get away with anything. They couldn't be trusted. His actions had proven that. A man like that—she couldn't build a life with.

Not caring which body part hurt, she flew out of the apartment faster than she'd moved in weeks. Within minutes, she was on the street and walking south. Hobbling down the steps of the 82nd Street subway entrance, she wiped her eyes and waited with dozens of commuters on the hot and crowded platform. The last time she'd been here, Dale had been by her side. It seemed like eons ago. She shook her head, trying to brush away the memory.

What was to become of the community center and Girls Up? The Starlight Ball was in ten days, and she'd expected to go with Dale to raise the needed funds. Clearly, that wasn't happening. Sylvia leaned against a pole and slumped.

Dale hadn't just ruined what they had between them. He'd destroyed the hopes and dreams of so many. Disaster didn't begin to cover what this was. His actions had hurt the people she loved, and it wasn't something she could ever forgive.

Chapter 25

Drumming his fingers on the leather seat, Dale stared blankly out the window as he and his driver waited in traffic on the West Side Highway. On his right, the Hudson River gleamed in the sunlight, and his stomach clenched as he remembered the day he and Sylvia sailed its waters. The day he'd admitted to himself, he was in love with her. Punching his fist onto the seat, he leaned back and willed the traffic to move.

A week had passed since Sylvia left his apartment. She'd ignored his calls and hadn't answered any of the dozens of texts he'd sent. He desperately wanted a chance to explain what had happened and to beg her forgiveness. If afterward, she still hated him, then he'd have to find a way to live with it.

As the car pulled up to his mother's East Seventy-Second Street townhouse, Candace Forester stood waiting in the open doorway at the top of the steps.

He climbed out of the car.

"How did it go, dear?"

"It's a bit complicated." Dale climbed the stairs to greet her. "I'm not sure I'll ever get over the fact the most powerful member of the Forester Industries Board of Directors, Oliver Banks, was behind all this."

His mother closed her eyes and shook her head. "Well, you better start from the beginning." She put her arm through his and ushered him through the foyer and into the spacious living room. "What happened?"

"Things didn't go as we'd hoped."

"Sit. Tell me everything," Candace said.

Dale sat opposite his mother and crossed his legs. "It took some time, and more than a few hours of negotiations between the lawyers from both sides, but we've managed to promise reparations for the Buffalo project. But it's going to cost us." He cleared his throat. "As for the Washington Heights development"—he let out a long sigh—"the mayor's decided he wants to reopen the bidding."

Candace Forester put a hand to her throat. "But why in heaven's name would he want to do that? We've already won the bid. The project has already begun. Please tell me there's nothing wrong."

The last thing Dale wanted was to give his mother more bad news. But she was a strong woman and a member of the board. She needed to know everything. Dale bit his lower lip. "Unfortunately, it turns out Oliver had his hands in this project, too. He arranged for a contract with the same cement supplier used in Buffalo—complete with kickbacks and sub-standard materials ready to be shipped."

"Oh, my goodness." Candace turned ashen. "But you didn't know about those contracts—did you?"

"Of course not," Dale said. "I mean, I suspected somcthing—that's why all the trips to Buffalo. And I had the accountants looking into the books. But I wanted to wait until I was sure we had solid evidence. Unfortunately, Oliver was clever, and we took too long to find out what was really going on. Then the story broke before we could handle the situation and make it right."

"Oh, honey." Candace leaned forward and put a hand over her son's. "It will be all right."

"No, Mother, it won't." Dale closed his eyes and bowed his head. The room felt as if it were closing in. He loosened his tie and unbuttoned his top button before he spoke again. "I'm the CEO of Forester Industries. I should have known what was going on in my own company. And the mayor agrees, which is why we have to re-bid and allow the city to audit our books. His exact words were, 'This happened under your watch. You need to prove yourself, son.' And, Mother, he's right. We all knew Oliver Banks was evil. We just never confronted it."

"Don't be so hard on yourself, darling." Candace fingered the pearls around her neck.

"No. I should have found a way to buy him out." Dale looked down and stared at the carpet. He was still reeling from his meeting with the mayor. It had been a wake-up call on so many levels. "I was too busy holding onto my job. In truth, I just thought he was power-hungry. I had no idea he wanted to bring us down and would do anything to make it happen, including paying someone to hurt—maybe even kill Sylvia Ramirez."

Candance blanched. "Kill? I don't understand. Why her, of all people."

Dale scoffed. "It gave him the perfect opportunity to eliminate the two biggest thorns in his side."

Candace tilted her head. "What do you mean, dear? How?"

"You know he never wanted to do anything but build luxury housing in Washington Heights. Oliver thought the people who actually lived in the neighborhood were disposable." Dale made a wide, sweeping motion with his hand. "Get rid of them, and gentrify the whole area. That was Oliver's plan." His voice rose. "And Sylvia Ramirez was in the way. So, he planted that initial article in the media about Forester Industries taking kickbacks, which of course we unknowingly were, because he was masterminding it all behind our backs. And if that wasn't enough, at the same time, he managed to convince corporate sponsors to bail out of the commitments they'd made to Sylvia's scholarship program." The whole situation gave him a sick feeling in his gut.

"He's a monster." Candace shivered.

"That's being kind." Dale ran a hand through his hair. "Never in a million years did Oliver think I'd grow a spine and join forces with Sylvia. So, he thought if he got rid of her, the project would certainly fail." He took a breath. "That, and the fact he planned to expose the kickbacks to the media. Which he did."

Dale stood, shoved his hands in his pockets, and paced. He'd spent the past twenty-four hours trying to wrap his head around all that had happened. Digesting the information wasn't easy. "Mother, I've never physically hurt anyone in my life, but the urge to do bodily damage to that man"—Dale clenched his fists—"it's a good thing he's in custody."

"When's the arraignment?" Candace asked.

"Tomorrow." Dale stepped over to one of the two tall windows facing the street. Leaning against the frame, he stared at the sun-dappled leaves of the red maple in front of the townhouse and tried to still his mind. Except for the acid churning in his stomach, it was a seemingly perfect summer day. "He'll be charged with racketeering and attempted murder." His voice was dull.

"Good. I hope he goes away for a very long time," Candace spoke with finality.

"So do I, Mother. But for now, we have another problem." He turned from the window. "If we lose the bid, who knows if another company will include a community center or scholarships? Those people were counting on us." He walked to the fireplace and leaned against the mantel. "I'm not sure what the next step is, but I don't want to wait to see what the mayor does, or if he accepts another bid."

"Oliver did more damage than he'll ever know."

"That he did," Dale said. "We need to move forward and do everything we can to earn back our good name and to make sure Washington Heights gets their community center, affordable housing, and keeps the Girls Up Scholarships going."

He closed his eyes and pinched the bridge of his nose. "At the end of the day, it doesn't matter that we didn't know what Oliver was doing. Forester Industries will take responsibility for the Buffalo site and the Washington Heights projects. At the company's expense, we'll tear down the faulty, sub-standard material and rebuild." Just saying those words out loud had the effect of a giant anvil being lifted from his chest. The revisions for each project would cost millions, but Dale was determined to make this right, no matter the cost.

"You did the right thing, dear, but now it's time to let our PR people take over and do their jobs."

Dale sighed. "Nah, let's not."

"For goodness sake, why not?"

"Because we should do the right thing without boasting about it or expecting any accolades. I say we move on and hope we do enough good that the public's perception changes."

"Son, you're a lot like your father." Candace smiled. "I'm proud of you."

"Thanks, Mother. That means a lot." Dale sat and blew out a breath.

"The worst of it is behind us. It's time to look ahead. And from where I sit, that means being a mother and letting you know that you don't look all that well, dear. You look as if you haven't had a decent meal in a while."

Dale groaned. "I've been too upset to eat."

Candace rose from her chair. "Now, none of that. I've asked Cook to make us something informal in the kitchen, and you, my dear, will have some nourishment. I won't have you getting sick." She motioned for him to get up. "Come along, now."

Dale followed his mother through the living room, past the formal dining room and the study on the left, and into the first-floor kitchen. Its far door led out onto a small patio. It had been a while since anyone had taken care of him, and until that moment, he hadn't realized how much he'd missed his mother's ministrations.

"We're ready, Margaret." Candace nodded to her cook.

Dale stepped out onto the patio and pulled out a wrought iron chair for his mother.

Once the lunch was served and they were alone, his mother wiped her mouth with a linen napkin and cleared her throat. "Now, what do you plan to do about

Sylvia?”

“What do you mean?” Dale looked down, hoping his mother hadn’t noticed the flush he felt on his cheeks at the mention of Sylvia.

“Oh, please.” Candace waved a hand. “I know you’ve been seeing her. She’s been living in your apartment, and I’ve never seen you happier. This entire situation must have upset her.”

Dale slumped in his chair. “She’s refusing my calls. She’s blocked me. She won’t answer my texts—it’s been radio silence.” He threw his napkin on the table. “Damnit, she’s wiped me from her universe and to tell the truth, it’s making me crazy in a way I’ve never experienced before.”

Candace laughed. “You need to stop with the dramatics and do something.”

“I don’t *know* what to do.”

“That’s not very imaginative.” Candace leaned across the table and took her son’s hands in her own. “If you’ve learned anything from your father, it’s that sometimes you have to fight for what you want in life. And if she’s who you want, you’ll have to fight to win her back because Sylvia is the type of woman who doesn’t accept anything less than everything you’ve got.”

A sudden relief washed over him, and he felt the clenched muscle in his jaw relax. His mother had the uncanny ability to get straight to the heart of the matter. Dale reached over and hugged her. “Thanks.”

“For what?”

“For always being there.” He kissed her on the cheek.

“Go now. Find her. Talk to her.” Candace smiled.

"I love you, and I'm proud of you. I have a good feeling this is all going to work out."

Dale sat back and let out a breath. He wished he felt as certain as his mother.

****

The knocking startled Sylvia awake. She lifted herself onto one elbow, looked around, and blinked several times. After weeks at Dale's home in the sky, waking up in her tiny apartment was disorienting.

The knocking persisted.

"Sylvia, are you in there? It's me," Randi called through the door. "I'm using my key, and I'm coming in."

Sylvia rubbed her eyes as Randi burst into the apartment.

"Gur-r-r-l-l-l! Jeez, I know you said you needed some alone time, but one week is too long to be holed up in this one room, ignoring the outside world." Randi threw open the curtains. She turned and sat next to where Sylvia lay on the fold-out couch. "There's so much you've missed, and I need to tell—"

"Randi, please. Stop. I'm not in the mood." Sylvia's voice sounded hoarse from crying.

"*Pobrecita,* you look wrecked. But no man is worth it."

"Rand-i-i-i-i-i-i." Sylvia had wanted to sound angry, but it came out more like a whine. She slapped her pillow. "Don't you get it? We've lost everything. Everything." Sylvia leaned forward. "I hate him, and everything he's done."

Randi's eyes widened. "Oh, honey, have you even brushed your teeth?" She made a fanning motion in front of her nose. "I can tell it's been a while. Come on,

Get up! Get up!"

"Leave me alone," Sylvia said.

"Not until you wash up, sweetie."

Sylvia tried to resist.

Randi grabbed her by the shoulders, lifted her off the couch, and marched her into the tiny bathroom.

Sylvia slumped onto the toilet seat.

"Oh, no, you don't. No sitting. Strip."

"Please go away." Sylvia pouted.

"Come on. You'll feel better once you get cleaned up. And then we need to talk." She turned on the bathtub faucets.

Sylvia took off her T-shirt and shorts.

"Whoa! I'm gonna have to burn those." Randi pointed to the pile of clothes now lying on the floor.

Sylvia slumped against the wall and cried. "I can't believe this has happened." She hiccupped through sobs. "I didn't just hurt myself. I let the whole neighborhood down."

"Don't be so hard on yourself. Take your bath and try to relax a little." Randi squeezed Sylvia's shoulder. "I'll get you some fresh clothes."

The small bathroom filled with steam, and Sylvia turned off the faucets. The hot water did look inviting, but her mind wouldn't shut off. How could she get through this heartbreak? How was she going to fix the situation with the community? All she wanted to do was crawl back into bed and forget she ever heard the name Forester.

With her booted foot hanging off the side of the tub, she soaked until her fingers were shriveled prunes. Finally, she resigned herself to the fact the situation was hopeless. Frustrated, she slapped at the now-tepid water, and got out of the tub. Randi was waiting when she'd finished dressing.

"Sit at the table," Randi said. "How have you been living this past week? There's no food in your refrigerator. I had to run downstairs to get that." She pointed to an egg sandwich sticking out of its aluminum foil. "Man, those five flights are a killer."

Sylvia unwrapped a paper straw, jabbed it through the plastic lid of an iced coffee, and sucked up a big swallow. "Thanks." She wiped her eyes.

"Eat. Then we're heading over to the hospital," Randi said.

"The hospital? What for?"

"I knew you forgot. Today's the day the doctor looks at your ankle and says you don't have to wear that boot anymore."

Putting her head down on the table, Sylvia began to cry again.

"I don't understand. That's a good thing. Why are you crying now?"

Sylvia held up her index finger as if to say, *give me a minute*. But she didn't move or speak. She sat with her head on the table, her arms over her head, and continued to sob.

"Honey, what's going on? You're worrying me."

Several minutes passed before Sylvia sat up, her hair askew, her eyes wet. She took in a shaky breath and hiccupped a sob. "I was so looking forward to getting rid of this damn boot because it meant I could go the Starlight Ball with Dale, and we'd dance and have a wonderful time, and I'd raise tens or even hundreds of thousands of dollars for the community center and the scholarship program, and now it's all ruined and…" She finally took a breath and then burst into tears again.

"Oh, sweetie." Randi handed Sylvia a paper napkin. "Blow your nose." She rubbed Sylvia's back. "Go ahead, get it all out. I'm giving you five more minutes for this pity party and then we're outta here. First to the hospital, then we're headed to the construction trailers."

"No, no, I can't go there. Too many memories and way too many failed dreams."

"Stop it. This isn't you talking. This is heartbreak talking, and you'll have to tell it to shut up. People are relying on us. Besides, there's some news I need to tell you. If you'd bothered to turn on your TV or turned your phone back on, you would know. Forester Industries isn't the big bad criminal they were made out to be."

Sylvia narrowed her eyes. "What are you talking about?"

Randi cracked her knuckles, put her forearms on the table, and leaned forward. "There's been a thorough investigation, and the Manhattan DA's office arrested Forester's big bad board member, Oliver Banks. Turns out, he was the brains behind all the kickbacks and other nasty stuff. He also hired people to move the steps in front of our work trailer and that's the reason you fell. He figured if he got you out of the way, Forester wouldn't have to build the community center. Banks hated the whole idea of it." Randi told Sylvia everything she knew, including the fact the city had re-opened the bidding process for the Washington Heights Development Project.

"Are you for real? Why wasn't that the first thing

you said when you walked in the door?" Sylvia was almost shouting.

"If you hadn't been boo-hoo'ing in your apartment this last week, you would have already heard. Besides, when I got here, a few hygiene matters needed to be handled on a priority basis."

Brushing her hair off her face, Sylvia blew a breath out through her nose. "I don't know what to say. I don't even know how I feel. I mean, I'm happy they got to the truth, but it doesn't absolve Dale. He's the CEO. He should have known. Because of him, we don't even know if we'll have a new community center, never mind the scholarship program."

"Wow." Randi's jaw dropped. "You've always been the optimist. What happened?"

"Dale Forester happened." Sylvia jabbed her finger in the air to make the point.

"I gotta believe there's still hope," Randi said.

"Now that the bidding is open again, who knows who'll win it? And if it's not Forester, there's bound to be another fight to get a new company to agree to build the things we need." Sylvia twisted her hair into a bun on top of her head. "Regardless of what happens, Dale Forester is never going to be in my life again. I've decided. We're just too different. I'm not from his world"—she held up a hand—"and don't say anything because I don't want to discuss it." She stood. "Come on. Let's go get this dang boot off."

Chapter 26

With the boot removed from her ankle, Sylvia enjoyed a physical lightness she hadn't felt in weeks, and it slightly lifted her mood. She even walked the ten blocks from the hospital to the work trailers. She hadn't been back since her accident, and nothing much had changed except for the new steps now securely bolted to their trailer.

The moment she stepped into her makeshift office, her heart sank. This place had once held so many possibilities. Now, it only served to remind her of broken promises. Sylvia followed Randi to the back room, tossed her purse on the desk, and sank into the chair. "Well, with everything up in the air, I'm not sure where to start. I guess I should gather all the paperwork, make sure it's—"

"Hello? Can I come in?" a voice from the front of the trailer called.

Sylvia and Randi responded simultaneously, "Who is it?"

"It's me, Luís."

"Of course, Luís, you're always welcome." Sylvia walked to the front, with Randi close behind.

With his hands in his pockets, Luís stood in the open doorway.

"Come on in," Sylvia said. "Is Carmen with you?"

"Well, I'm not exactly alone. I'm not sure we're all

going to fit," Luís said.

Sylvia raised her eyebrows. "What do you mean?"

Luís stepped aside.

Sylvia looked past him. At least fifty people from the neighborhood were standing in front of the trailer, taking up every inch of available space. Not a smiling face could be found.

"We came to ask you what's going on," Luís explained. "We haven't been able to get answers from the building committee or the mayor's office."

"Yeah, you're the only one that's going to tell it to us straight," a man in the back of the group yelled.

The rest of the crowd nodded.

"We've taken out loans to buy store space in the new buildings," Juan from the dry cleaners said. "And the store owners on Broadway have paid for new awnings and signage. What happens to those investments if there aren't going to be any new buildings?"

"What about the community center?" Gabriel from the bike store asked.

"And the Girls Up program?" A woman's voice spoke up from the back of the crowd. "My daughter was counting on that."

The air hummed with tension as more people gathered, the mood shifting from nervous curiosity to anger. Sylvia didn't like where this was heading.

"Dang, people. We're not the enemy," Randi shouted over the mingled voices. "Let's let Sylvia talk. She'll tell you what's going on."

Giving Randi a sideways glance, Sylvia inched her way forward onto the top step of the trailer and faced the mass of people. Having no idea what to say, she cleared her throat, stalling for time. The people of the neighborhood had every right to know what was happening. Their livelihoods, which they'd spent years building, were being threatened. She'd dragged the entire community into the fight against Forester Industries. Who else would they come to for answers? Why hadn't she just let the entire situation go? Never gotten involved with Dale. Never gotten her heart broken, her trust betrayed, and her community enflamed. She waved her hands to get their attention. "Okay, everyone. Please. Let's calm down."

The crowd silenced and looked at her.

Sylvia pressed her lips together and took in a deep breath. She hoped the next words out of her mouth would be the right ones.

****

Dale had been relieved when Mayor Simms agreed to see him on such short notice. The big surprise was the mayor's swift acceptance of Dale's proposal for Forester Industries to continue work on the Washington Heights project rather than starting from scratch with a new company. Of course, there'd been the proverbial slap on the wrist, and Dale had to promise things he wouldn't normally give away—but it was worth it. Regardless of the reason for the mayor's turnabout, it had worked out better than Dale had expected or hoped. The hint of a skip was even in his step as he left the mayor's office to head uptown to the construction site. Now all he needed to do was figure out a way to win Sylvia back. "Take the West Side Highway north," Dale told his driver when he got into the car.

"Sorry, Mr. Forester, it's closed until Fifty-Third Street. Construction. Traffic's a mess. Nothing's moving."

"Damn." The last thing he wanted to do was wait in traffic. "Okay, never mind. I'm getting out." He loosened his tie and slipped off his jacket, then opened the car door and headed for the subway.

By the time Dale reached the platform, his shirt felt as if it were glued to his body. The horrific New York City humidity, coupled with the thought that Sylvia might reject him, had Dale sweating as if he'd run a marathon in the desert. Of course, she had every right to cut him out of her life and never speak to him again. But he hoped with the new decision for Forester to continue with the building, it would mitigate enough of the damage he'd caused and she could forgive him.

Twenty minutes later, he was on the street, walking briskly toward his destination. His heart beat like a jackhammer as he entered Sylvia's apartment building. He climbed the five flights and knocked on her door several times, but there was no response. His heart sank as he pressed his forehead against the door. Not certain if she wasn't home or was merely avoiding him, he began knocking again. "Sylvia, it's me, Dale. Look, I know you don't want to speak to me, but if you're in there, please open the door. I need to tell you something." The sound of a door opening at the other end of the hall made him turn.

"Shhhh! My baby is asleep. Sylvia's not home. Go away."

"Do you know where she is?"

A slammed door was the only response. Taking a deep, frustrated breath, he headed back down the stairs. "Where could she be?" No sooner had the words left his mouth than he knew exactly where to find her.

Back on the street, he crossed Broadway and jogged down 178th Street toward the river. He had no clue what he'd say to Sylvia, but the first thing he needed to do was ask for her forgiveness. Short of that, at least the chance to tell her what had really happened. She needed to know he'd had nothing to do with the bribes and kickbacks.

As he got closer to the construction site, he saw Randi headed toward him. He slowed and stopped in front of her, breathing hard.

"I didn't expect to see *you* here." Her eyebrows rose.

"Yeah, I know. Look, I need to speak to Sylvia, and she's not taking my calls or answering my texts."

"Sorry, but you're dead to her." Randi folded her arms across her chest and narrowed her eyes.

Dale flinched, the words hitting him like a punch to the gut. "I know she's upset—"

"Upset?" Randi sneered. "You are so clueless, man. She's had enough of you. Because of you, the people in the neighborhood are turning on her."

How could that be? He took a shaky step back. "What exactly do you mean?"

"You see that mob over there?" She pointed down the block to the growing crowd gathered behind the chain link fence in front of Sylvia's trailer. "That mob wants to know what she'll do about the fact they've taken out loans to lease space in a building *you're* not building. And they wanna know what's going to replace their community center, the one that *you* tore down."

"Look, I've got good news, and I need to tell her personally. Then if she wants to hate me for the rest of my life, well, okay, I deserve that. But at least she needs to hear me out."

Randi blew out a breath and shook her head. "I have no idea why I'm doing this…but…okay…I'm on my way to meet Miguel at *La Cocina*. Sylvia managed to get everyone to stop yelling and listen, so I'm picking up coffee and cakes so we can have a nice community meeting. Help me"—she gave a rueful smile—"and I'll personally bring you into the lion's den."

The idea of walking into a group of angry residents with legitimate complaints wasn't exactly what he had in mind. But if that's what it took to win back Sylvia, and make things right, then he knew he didn't have a choice. Dale swallowed hard and swept his hand to the side in an *after you* fashion. "Lead the way."

****

Sylvia managed to convince the crowd to consider approaching the mayor and suggest finding a new company who could continue with the plans already in motion. But they were getting restless. She checked her watch, wondering what was keeping Randi and Miguel with the refreshments. When she looked up, she saw them turning into the construction site with Dale Forester. Her eyes widened as she leaned forward, not believing what she was seeing.

A hush fell as heads turned to follow her gaze.

"Okay, people, we got coffee and almond cookies," Randi spoke loud enough to be heard over the crowd.

Sylvia stared at Dale as he helped wheel in a cart holding two large coffee urns and a supply of to-go cups, sugar, cream, cookies, and napkins. Refreshments were handed out as he worked his way toward her. The closer he got, the farther she stepped back, her mind telling her to flee. She turned, headed up the steps, and was about to enter the trailer when she heard Dale shout.

"Don't go! Please, Sylvia. Please. We need to talk."

Sylvia turned to see him inching toward her. "Stop." She held up her hand. "If you have something to say, go ahead. I think all these people would like to hear it, too." She crossed her arms over her chest and watched as Dale looked around at the gathered faces, perspiration forming on his upper lip. "We're listening."

Dale cleared his throat, every eye now on him.

Silence enveloped the crowd as they waited for Dale to speak.

Sylvia hoped they couldn't hear her heart, as it beat like a herd of thundering horses. He looked tired, with at least two days of stubble on his face, and yet, he was still gorgeous. But how could she forget he'd broken her heart and let down the whole community? He had something to say, and she felt certain it would either rock her world or wreck her day. She wasn't sure she wanted to wait around for the outcome.

Dale pressed his lips together and shoved his hair off his forehead. "Sylvia, I want to apologize for all you've had to go through. Because the only reason you were hurt was because someone was trying to get to me."

On impulse, Sylvia took a step back.

"Wait." Dale held up a hand. "I'm not saying this right. Let me see if I can explain." He paused and bit his lower lip. "Oliver Banks was an evil man. And he was on our board. He's the one who hired a couple of guys to move these steps, which resulted in your injuries. He thought he could get me to stop building if you were out of the way. I guess he didn't realize I wanted this project almost as much as you and the people in the neighborhood. You probably know he's been arrested, but I'll never forgive myself for what happened."

The crowd eyed him closely, but no one spoke.

Sylvia remained silent.

Dale took in a breath. "Over the last couple of months, I've come to love this community—The Heights. I've learned a lot about the people who live here. I've gotten to see them through your eyes and witness all the good work you do. And, well…I just couldn't take the chance that another developer wouldn't do the right thing by you all."

Sylvia's breath hitched. "What are you saying?" She saw dozens of cold eyes staring at Dale, as people began to shout.

"What did you do, man?"

"What's going to happen to us?"

"Did you take another bribe?"

"Listen, all of you." Dale turned to them, holding up his hands. "Please let me finish."

Taking a step forward, Sylvia nodded. "Come on, folks, let's hear what he has to say."

When they quieted down, Dale spoke. "Forester Industries will be building the new Washington Height Development," Dale shouted, "and it will include a new community center and a scholarship program, as promised. Everything is moving ahead as originally planned."

The crowd erupted in cheers, with neighbors

hugging neighbors.

"How? How did this happen?" Sylvia called out above the jubilation. "I thought it was being opened up to other bids."

The crowd quickly went silent and dozens of faces turned toward Dale.

Putting his hands in his pockets, Dale rocked back on his heels. "I had to make a few promises to the city." He paused and gave a sly smile. "Like a new park and a few other concessions."

Sylvia couldn't believe what she was hearing. "You did that for us?" She put her hands over her heart. Dale's smile was so wide her heart melted.

He turned to look at the crowd, who had been hanging on his every word. "Folks, I wish I could say I did it for all of you. But that's not exactly true." He spun to face Sylvia. "Because I did it for her."

She shook her head. *Did I hear that right?* "Me?" Dale walked up the steps until he was so close she could feel his breath.

"Yes, for you because I love you, Sylvia Ramirez. Right here, in front of everyone, I'll say it—*te quiero, mi amor.*"

Happy tears welled up behind her eyes, and her knees went weak. Undisturbed by the cat calls, whistles, and cheers from the crowd, Sylvia returned Dale's embrace and whispered in his ear, "Oh, Dale, I love you, too!" And when she felt his lips press against hers, she closed her eyes and melted into his kiss. She was exactly where she wanted to be—in love and in Dale's embrace.

Epilogue

Twelve Months Later—The Plaza Hotel—The Starlight Charity Ball

Sylvia breathed in the perfume-filled air. "Wow, they really pulled out all the stops." She scanned the ballroom decorated with dozens of round tables all covered with gold-trimmed tablecloths, topped with centerpieces filled with white roses and exotic orchids. The dance floor featured expensively dressed couples swaying to the sounds of a live orchestra.

Several photographers snapped photos while guests strolled from one table to another, greeting each other with air kisses. White-jacketed waiters moved effortlessly through the crowd, filling crystal champagne glasses.

Smiling, Sylvia squeezed Dale's arm. "Ready?"

"Ready," he said.

They descended the steps to join the others at their table.

Her shoulders relaxed, even as they made their way through the crush of some of the wealthiest people on the East Coast.

"Did I tell you how beautiful you look tonight?"

"Uh-huh."

"In this room, you're a standout. Hands down, the most beautiful—" Dale stopped and tugged on her arm.

"You haven't heard a word I've said."

"Huh?"

"Sylvia?"

"Yes, Dale?"

"I think I know why you're not listening to me proclaim the miracle of your beauty. It's because you're mentally calculating how many more computers you'll be able to buy after tonight."

His last remark caught her attention. "How'd'ya know?"

He put his arm around her, pulling her in close. "Because I know how that mind of yours works, and it's only one of the many reasons why I love you." He kissed her on the temple. "If I had to guess, I'd imagine you'll be able to not only outfit the entire computer room, but even get a separate, dedicated satellite dish."

A smile spread across Sylvia's face. "I like the way you think."

The grand opening of the new Washington Heights Community Center would take place in two weeks. After a year of planning, hard work, and a few compromises, the center featured nearly everything Sylvia had wanted, including a community garden and a gymnasium. She was ecstatic.

Dale had proven he was as good as his word. In fact, he'd moved mountains to make room for the list of Sylvia's *must-haves*, and she'd agreed to do all the fundraising for the necessary furniture, computers, sports equipment, art supplies, and gardening tools. In the last year, she and Randi raised more than half of what they needed. But tonight's affair would allow them to complete their money hunt.

"Come on. We're over there." Dale pointed to a

large table in the center of the room.

She caught a glimpse of Randi waving. When they reached the table, Candace Forester rose and kissed Sylvia on both cheeks.

"How's my future daughter-in-law, and what held you two up?"

"We stopped by the community center for a few minutes." Sylvia placed her sequined clutch on the table.

"Whatever for?" Candace asked.

"Sylvia wanted one last look at the paint chips in a different light." Dale shook his head and chuckled.

"I thought we settled on the paint colors yesterday." Randi raised an eyebrow.

"We did, but, unfortunately, that was yesterday. Today, Sylvia had a different idea." Dale shrugged.

"Okay, okay. So, I changed my mind." Sylvia put her hands on her hips.

"Again?" Candace and Randi chimed in unison.

They all laughed.

"I know. I know. I just want it to be perfect." Sylvia batted her lashes and sat.

Randi reached over and touched Sylvia's arm. "Relax. It *will* be perfect."

Sylvia looked at the faces of her friends. "I just thought we should go with a lighter shade of blue, something a bit more soothing. And now I'm sure it's the exact right color." She sat a little straighter. "Anyway, on the way over I sent an email with our final choices to the painters. They start tomorrow, so, I can't make any more changes."

"Amen." Randi clasped her hands in a prayerful pose.

Candace nodded.

Sylvia leaned toward Randi. “What happened to the gray dress? It was smoking hot.”

“I’ll admit, I looked killer in it.” Randi sighed. “But every time I passed a mirror, the color reminded me of a funeral procession.”

“Oh, stop. It did not.” Sylvia slapped her playfully on the arm.

“No, for real. So, I thought I’d go with something a little more festive.”

“Well, that purple really catches the eye, and it’s color coordinated with your hair. I like it.”

“You think?”

“Yes. I think. You look amazing.”

“Thanks. But enough about my dress and the center. Give me all the deets on the apartment. Did you guys finally agree on the kitchen appliances?”

Sylvia pouted slightly. “No.”

“No?” Randi raised an eyebrow and shook her head at the same time.

“I gave up. Between the final touches on the center, getting ready for this ball, and decorating a new apartment all by myself, I finally had to admit that Dale was right. I should let a professional decorator take over.”

“You. Did. Not.” Randi smacked her hand on the table.

“Oh, don’t worry.” Sylvia put up her hand. “I still have the final say.”

“That’s my girl.” Randi lifted her champagne glass in a salute.

A slight tap on her shoulder had Sylvia turning to find Candace leaning toward her.

"Sylvia, I'd like you to meet an old college friend of Dale's." Candace pointed toward a tall, attractive man with sandy-colored hair, standing at the table. "This is Cody Woodbridge."

"I hear congratulations are in order." Cody smiled and gave Sylvia a half bow.

She looked up at a tall man and dark eyes. Sylvia self-consciously twisted the emerald-cut, seven-carat diamond on her left hand. "Thank you," she said. "And this is my friend and colleague, Randi Gomez."

"Hello," Cody said.

Randi smiled.

"It's nice to meet you, Ms. Gomez." Cody gave a slight bow of his head. "I understand you two ladies have a special cause for which you're interested in raising funds." He cocked his head. "Something about scholarships for girls, is it?"

Sylvia couldn't help but notice his laser-beam attention focused on Randi. Randi must have noticed it too because, surprisingly, her best friend seemed to be at a loss for words.

Cody crossed behind Sylvia and stood directly in front of Randi, offering his hand. "Would you care to tell me all about it while we dance?"

In all the years Sylvia had known Randi, she'd never seen her flustered, let alone blushing like she was now. But the sparks between the two were undeniable.

Randi seemed to squirm in her chair. "Uh. Okay."

Sylvia silently chuckled, watching her friend slowly take Cody's hand as he escorted her to the dance floor.

"You know he's worth more money than we are?" Dale whispered in Sylvia's ear. "And he really needs a tax shelter."

"Oh, goodie." Sylvia smiled at the prospect of some major funding for Girls Up. "This night just keeps getting better and better."

Later that night, they all squeezed into Dale's chauffeured stretch limo and headed uptown to *La Cocina*. Alma and Luís were holding a private, late-night party to celebrate Dale and Sylvia's engagement and the completion of the community center.

"Where are we headed?" Cody asked.

"To the best Puerto Rican restaurant in New York City," Dale said. "You're gonna love it."

Sylvia laughed and rested her head on Dale's shoulder.

He lifted her chin with his hand. "I love you, Sylvia Ramirez."

Sylvia stared into his eyes and slowly smiled. "I know."

"And I'm going to keep telling you how much I love you every day for the rest of our lives."

Sylvia let out a throaty laugh. "I know."

Dale leaned in and kissed her.

Sylvia sighed into his kiss. She was happier than she'd ever been. And as the kiss deepened, she knew they would spend the rest of their days together.

A word about the author...

Maria Lokken has spent the last couple of decades writing and producing in the world of reality television—where steel armor is preferable over cashmere sweater and pearls.

An avid reader of all genres, romance is where her heart lies. When not reading, or writing, she can be found eating whatever delectable goodie her wanna-be chef husband has prepared.

Thank you for purchasing
this publication of The Wild Rose Press, Inc.

For questions or more information
contact us at
info@thewildrosepress.com.

The Wild Rose Press, Inc.
www.thewildrosepress.com

CPSIA information can be obtained
at www.ICGtesting.com
Printed in the USA
BVHW050717280523
664999BV00013B/496